FALLEN
REALITY

FALLEN
REALITY

AVINASH DASHWIN

PARTRIDGE

To order additional copies of this book, contact
Toll Free 800 101 2657 (Singapore)
Toll Free 1 800 81 7340 (Malaysia)
orders.singapore@partridgepublishing.com

www.partridgepublishing.com/singapore

CONTENTS

CHAPTER 1

ESCAPING REALITY

"QUICK, WE'RE LOSING HIM". Those words imprinted on my thoughts as I was rushed somewhere on a bed with wheels.

My mind was running with thoughts and words while my body was filled with pain and blood as if I was involved in an accident that caused me to be in this serious condition. I could only see a bright light and some faces that I didn't recognize.

They were wearing scrubs with white lab coats on them. It felt cold as if my body was exposed to a certain degree of cold temperature that could almost cause a frostbite but my head felt warm and cozy with some kind of liquid running down my head.

A woman with glasses leaned closer to me while the bed was being pushed by some people "WE ARE ALMOST THERE PLEASE JUST STAY WITH US AND HANG IN THERE" whispered the woman. They all seemed worried about something. The woman's eyes were filled with tears and anger as those tears dripped upon me.

How could that two emotions combine, sadness and anger as if it was a very complicated situation that she does not know what to say or what to do. As the bed stopped moving, a bright light shone upon me. My head was in pain I was on the urge on giving up but then I heard three familiar voices "HANG IN THERE MAXIEL, IT'S NOT YOUR TIME YET".

Those voiced was filled with hope and love when I heard those voices, some kind of liquid was coming out of my eyes, it hurts yet it makes me feel happy. "What is this feeling, it makes my heart pound so hard and what's this stuff that's coming out of my eyes, am…am I cr…crying?

WHY? WHAT AM I CRYING ABOUT" I thought to myself? I heard a few movements as I was in the room as though as they were preparing for something important. A woman in a lab coat came closer holding a large needle filled with colorless liquid and she pierced it in a bag filled with liquid in a transparent bag.

In a few seconds, I felt very sleepy and then everything went dark as if I was brought to a place filled with darkness and despair but for some reason I kept on holding on to those voices it gave me hope, courage and all kinds of feelings that I could not describe. As things went dark, I could hear some noises around me as if I was on surgery and they put me on anesthetic "maybe that's what happening right now, I wonder what have I gotten myself into right now" I thought to myself.

"WE ARE LOSING HIM" a voice filled with despair and sadness filled my head. At that moment I was being very analytical but then something told me to stop overthinking and just relax. Then a song came upon my head that made me smile, it seems very familiar yet I could not remember the name. I know it's my favourite song yet I could not remember, how ironic.

At that moment I just went with the flow and relaxed while the song was filling my head with positive things. Then, everything went dark as I was being pulled away from reality and being dragged upon a bright place filled with hope and dreams. As I was brought in closer, I started to smile and was filled with warm and happy thoughts. The place was so bright and a hand was waving at me, trying to pull me closer. I went closer and closer as the heartwarming thoughts filled my head, I felt like a giant burden had been lifted of my shoulders.

"THIS IS JUST THE BEGINNING" said the voice. The voice was so smooth that it filled me with warmth as if I was being hugged and told that there were no more problems so I should stop overthinking and just enjoy the flow. I was then dragged up some place filled with darkness and despair. I was kind of between the light and the dark and a familiar voice came upon me "It's time to wake up", I was shocked by the voice as it felt like I was electrocuted. I moved towards the voice ignoring those places. As I moved towards that voice a bright light blinded me. My eyelids were really heavy at that moment but for some reason I knew that I do not have a choice. As I opened my eyes, I was blinking rapidly trying to adjust my eyes to the bright light, someone was sitting at the edge of the bed.

"Dude you got to wake up if you don't want to be late for school. Ooh … I knew that voice, it was Light. He is a close friend of mine. "Come on wake up, we are going to miss the bus". "H…HOW DID YOU GET IN HERE? I asked in a grumpy voice. "I climbed up your window … Oh! and remembered you have football practice after school", he replied while rolling his eyes. "Just give me a few more minutes, pleaseeeee", I was begging for time but I knew that he wouldn't easily give up. He started pulling my blankets from me. Thank god, I was wearing an undershirt and my boxers at that time. It looks like I have no choice, Light knows that I don't like the cold so by yanking my blankets off me, I have no choice but to get ready since I don't like being exposed to cold temperature. Light waited in my room while reading his psychology books, YES, he is interested in psychology. He has the ability to read people like an open book. I was brushing my teeth when I heard him yawning. "Hah! you're also tired aren't you? why must they put school in the morning, why can't they put it in the afternoon or at night? I asked Light while holding my toothbrush on my right hand and the toothpaste on the other.

"Well apparently, schools are put in the morning cause that's when our brains function and it's when we are fresh at that time, at least that's what they told us but I doubt it. Looking at our generation, it's best to put it at night since that's the time most of us are active for some reason, though. By the way, why am I answering your question at this time, could you hurry? He replied, while holding his book below his chin in a frustrated way.

"FINE, I would hurry". I quickly took a shower and went down for breakfast, I invited Light down for breakfast but he declined. As we got down of the stairs, I saw my mom making us breakfast, it's bacon and eggs.

"Ohhh, Hi Light, did you climb up Maxiel's window again, you could always use the front door you know".

"Yes, Miss Greene, I prefer the window, it's fun and adventurous".

"Don't forget it's also illegal since you are invading people's privacy and property" I replied.

Light just smirked at me and said "well you certainly have no privacy in your case Max, cause I know and will know everything about you", Light stated. I looked at him and rolled my eyes in an ignorant way. "Well then would you like to join us for breakfast before the bus came? I made eggs and bacon" my mom told Light in an inviting manner.

My mom thinks Light is a good example of a friend to me and I could not blame her. Frankly speaking I do like Light, he is always around when I needed someone to talk to and always there to help out, he's also my personal therapist cause he advises me a lot and his advises actually work. For example, one time I had trouble making friends with people in my school, he advised me the way to talk and told me to always be myself because there isn't any use if you make friends while being a faker. Light and me are like complete opposites of each other. I am the one active in sports while he is the smart one, he always comes in the top three in our school but he doesn't brag about it, he is still humble unlike certain people that I know, that is one of the reasons that I liked him as a friend.

"Umm… no thanks Miss Greene, I had my breakfast just now". "Just a little, I kind of owe you since you are the one who is always waking my Max up for school" my mom insisted and when she does, she will never take no as an answer. Light knew that there was no way out so he just accepted. My mom really had her way with people. She always try to provide the best for me even though she is always busy with work. She is a doctor and she takes her job very seriously especially after my dad died. My mom couldn't save my dad in time that is why she now takes her job seriously so that no one would suffer the same fate as we did. While at breakfast we were having little talks about school, teachers and my football practice. The bus will be arriving in five minutes' time so I said goodbye to my mom and dragged Light to the porch of the house. "Goodbyyyee… Miss Greene and thanks for the breakfast" said Light while I was dragging him to the porch. "MY…MY where are you guys going off in a hurry" she laughed with a smirk while removing her glasses.

As I dragged Light up to the porch, I pulled up my blue jacket and put in onto my grey long sleeve shirt. "So why did you drag me here?" Light asked politely, he seemed worried as though I was going to scold or yell at him. One thing that I noticed about Light is that sometimes he has anxiety issues, his brain will always try to figure out stuff and outcomes that will happen. "Relax, I just wanted us to reach in time for the bus, even though I always wake up late but I am still punctual about my timing and stuff", I replied reassuringly to him. "We could be there a little while you know to enjoy the heat, instead we are out here five minutes early on the edge of getting frostbite". He then took out a black jacket with hoodie and wore it upon his orange shirt. I looked at his attire and it really matches him. "Dude you could really pull this off with that faded jeans and those black sneakers, it really suites you. You must have taken a long time to figure out those combinations of clothing didn't you?" I asked. "PFTTT!… not really, I just took the first thing out of my drawer, as long as it's clean and good. You should stop over analyzing stuff" he smirked but in a cunning way yet calm. How do people combine two opposite and unmixable emotions together, that, must be some kind of talent. As I was going through my thoughts, suddenly a yellow vehicle pulled over and honed. I was shocked by the honk. Guess I do tend to overthink sometimes.

"Looks like, someone isn't paying attention to his surroundings." Light smirked again.

I guess he must have known that I was overthinking stuff again. I hate it when he is right, it's like he is hiding something from me. At the moment I feel a bit uneasy as if something is wrong somewhere. Why do I feel this way? Why am I overthinking stuff? Why am I feeling uneasy? "YOU GETTING IN KID?" said a man with spiky hair and pale face. He was wearing a blue collar shirt with a jacket upon it and he has dark blue slacks too. He was driving the bus, of course he is the bus driver. Why am I looking at the attire of the bus driver as if my brain is telling me that there is something wrong or something weird that is going on around here. WHY AM I THINKING SO CRITICALLY AND OVER ANALYZING STUFF RIGHT NOW? I took a deep breath and replied to the man in the blue collar shirt "Yeaahhhhhhhhhh… sorry for that" I replied in a humble manner and climbed upon the bus. "I apologize for my friend there, he likes to daydream and overthink stuff a lot" said Light.

"Seems like you have issues, you need a counselor", said the man in the blue collar shirt while looking at my direction.

"WRONG, HE NEEDS GOD THAT'S WHAT HE NEEDS" shouted a brunette girl with ponytail who was wearing a pink shirt with a pink jacket upon it and black jeans. Her freckled face was filled with smirk.

"Hey NATASHA" Light smiled at her in a friendly and inviting tone. "Get in, I don't want you kids to be late for school" said the man with blue collared shirt. Light and I headed towards our normal seat which was in the fourth row towards the left. Behind the seat, there was a girl with blonde hair and green highlights. She was wearing a purple sweater with a picture of a horse and a turquoise color scarf that goes along with it. She seems familiar and then it clicked to me, its JEAN…. JEAN DORSON, my childhood friend. Why did it take a long time for me to recognize her? Maybe my head was running with thoughts and that I needed time to process certain information including her looks and her attire in order to be recognized. I should really stop overthinking stuff for my own sake, it's really troubling. When we are heading towards our seats, she smiled at me. That smile was filled with warmth and welcome. When we took a seat, she immediately gave me a hug from behind. I was shocked. "Hey there Greene how was your weekend?" she asked excitedly. Her face was filled with cheer and happiness as though it was the best moment of her life.

"HEY JEAN, HOW ARE YOU?" I asked politely.

Light was sitting near the window where he always sat so, he could enjoy the view while I was sitting beside him while turning my head towards Jean and giving her my full attention. Jean is really a good friend and also a good person, she is an optimistic person, kind and also one of the most friendliest person in our school. The truth is that's what worries me the most, I have read one of Light's psychology book and it says that the person who has the brightest smile and looks cheerful all the time is most probably the person who has the most problems and are probably suffering from depression. The reason they choose to be happy and cheerful in front of other people is to make sure that the person doesn't have the same problems as they do. Apparently, they are also one of the best people to ask advise for, this made me think the wonderful person Jean is, who always helped me through thick and thin but what have I ever done for her as a sign of all the help and kindness that she has given me. Jean is very good in interacting with people, that's her gift. She is also the life of the party and she has a high social status but then again I am worried about what I have read, maybe I am overthinking too much. Looking at Jean, I mean come on it's really hard to believe that with the childish and innocent smile of hers could actually be hiding a deep and dark secret such as loneliness and depression.

"Jean if you need anything I am here for you" I said politely. Light and Jean looked towards me with their jaw wide open as though they could not believe what they have heard.

"Wow that was really unexpected, umm…. Thanks Max, I am also here for you if you need me I guess" Jean replied with an awkward laugh.

"HMM… I agreed with Jean, that is so unusual of you today. Is everything okay? Light asked.

"Yeah, I just need more sleep" I replied.

Throughout the whole journey I realized that Jean and Light had made a lot of eye contact. It seemed like they were hiding something. There was silence for a while until Jean broke the silence. "Hey are you guys going to Elle Sanderson seventeenth birthday party this weekend". Light and I looked at each other as I was about to say no, Light suddenly said "We will be there". I looked at Light irritatingly. "I know you don't like parties and all but maybe this could help you a bit since you keep on looking troubled since this morning, you need to relax. Plus, this could boost your social status too, I have never heard of an antisocial football player such as yourself", Light told me in a polite manner. I think he is right, maybe this could be good for me. As I was looking towards Light, I noticed something in the background. It was a girl. She has long blonde hair and bright yellow eyes. She was fair and she was wearing a bright white dress. She started waving and smiling towards me as the bus passed by. It was in a flash but I managed to pick up her image, maybe my conscience got a peek at her. Anyway, as soon as we reached our destination Jean tapped me on the shoulder signaling that we have reached our destination. I got up from my seat and exited the bus but as I did that I heard someone said "NOW, DON'T YOU FORGET ABOUT THAT COUNSELLOR THOUGH". It was the guy in the blue collar shirt also known as the bus driver who thought that I have some issues. That is sure a good way to start the morning. Jean pulled me and Light out of the bus as we waved goodbye to the driver.

CHAPTER 2

HIDDEN CHARACTERS

As we arrived at our destination which is also known as the place where hopes and dreams are questioned and ruled by a system. At least that is what I kept on calling it but other people call it school. Welcome to DENFORD HIGH where everyone tries to fit in.

"Hey guys, have you done your Biology homework yet" Jean asked desperately. "Let me guess' you forgot to do it and you want to borrow ours, am I right?" Light asked, questioning Jean.

As Jean and Light continued talking about our biology assessment, I was shocked as I saw the same girl with the white dress. It's really cold and I am questioning why is she wearing a white dress during a cold weather but,it really suites her. She looked towards me with a smile. At that point I immediately asked Light and Jean whether do they know the girl that I was pointing at but they did not look in time cause when a green truck passed by, she suddenly vanished. "Guess someone has started hallucinating in the morning huh, did you take any wrong medication Max or did you take a little booze this morning?" Jean asked teasingly.

Light looked at the direction, I was pointing too and he was confused.

"I think you just saw something, maybe because you're still too sleepy, come on I will accompany you to wash your face".

"By the way could I still borrow your homework guys, please" Jean kept on insisting.

"Fine, fine just make sure to give it back later before Mrs Egertson class okay" Light finally gave in.

Light placed his bag on the grass and took out his Biology homework and hand it to Jean. Jean is really good with her social status and all that but she is also bad at managing her time but I don't blame her though because once you reach a point of popularity or fame in the school, I am pretty sure that she has consistency to keep her status up. Plus Jean has helped me and Light countless times. For example, when I had to help Mr Gilmert in some physics stuff, I had football practice that day, Jean willingly volunteered to help Mr Gilmert so that I could attend my practice or when the time where Light had a terrible flu, Jean brought some chicken soup to his house and served it to him even though she has tons of homework. In a way, she is kind of selfless because she put others before her own self and that's why I like her as my friend. As she took Light's homework and went, Light dragged me into the school hall.

"Okay you have to tell me what is wrong, you seem a bit off today" Light asked insistingly that I should tell him.

"I think I might be a bit sleepy and aren't you the one that could read people like an open book?" I replied to Light with a sense of sarcasm. "What did you meant earlier when you pointed at something that you claimed to be a girl?" Light was still insisting.

"Ugh… I don't know, why do you want to know anyway?" I questioned him back.

"I just want you to be safe, just be careful okay, could you at least describe her to me" Light asked politely.

"Well she has long blonde hair with bright yellow eyes. OHHH! and she also wore a white dress". As soon as I told Light about that he sighed in relief. That was the confusing part, at first he kept on insisting that I should have told him and now he sighed in relief. I looked at him with a lifted eyebrow, questioning him of his reactions. He looked up at me and sighed in relief "Thank god, now I know you are really hallucinating since no one would wear a dress during a cold weather".

"Maybe you are right, I think I am just tired" I replied.

We headed towards our locker to take out our books. Light's locker was just beside mine, no it wasn't a coincidence. I asked the principal a favor to do so because it is easier for me to get our work done and hand it in but the most important reason is that Light actually helped me to keep my locker tidy. It would be a real mess if it hadn't been for Light's assistance.

We trust each other with our locker's combination in case if there is any emergency but the real reason is that, I need his help in order to keep my locker tidy. Without him, I think there will be piles of garbage and stuff there. I took out my schedule

"This is going to be a long day" I sighed. As I was about to put back my schedule, I saw a picture of the girl in the white dress. I freaked out as I saw that picture. Light must have noticed my reaction

"Hey is everything alright?" he asked.

"Yeah, I am alright. Hey, Light what do you see in this picture?" I asked.

He took it out of my hand and said "All I see is a pizza coupon you got here". I looked again and it was really just a pizza coupon.

That's it maybe I am going crazy. I think I am just tired that's all.

"YOU MUST BE TIRED" Light said with a sigh. WHY IS THIS HAPPENING TO ME??? Light looked at me "Come on if you want to talk, let's talk over this during recess, we have to head to our chemistry class now". I shook my head, agreeing to Light's idea but right now my head is going through a lot of questions, like who is that girl? Is she a ghost or just someone who is just trying to prank me? As I was heading towards chemistry class with Light, I felt strange as though I have done this before but I chose to ignore the feeling. There is this door that connects us directly to our chemistry class.

Light twisted the doorknob and let me in first, then he closed it as he entered the class. Our chemistry teacher was quite strict and kind of a perfectionist. Her name is Mrs. Kina. She might be strict but there are times where she is cool, that is if we do all her homework and listen to her lectures without any distractions. She is the main reason I got easily stressed up on chemistry. "OKAY CLASS SETTLE DOWN, TODAY WE ARE GOING TO LEARN ABOUT ALKENES AND

ALKANES SO EVERYONE PARTNER UP IN TWO" Mrs. Kina ordered.

Well it was obvious that I am always going to be partners with Light. As everyone else searched for their partners, Light and I were going over the instruction manual of the experiment that we are conducting. Well long story short, we aced it even though Light did most of the work but I did help out too, in my own ways like taking the stuff and all those simple stuff.

Our next class was English Literature …Oh God, that's the time where I think about my life decisions and regrets. Don't get me wrong, I don't hate English Literature, it is just that our teacher [MRS EGERTSON] is kind of boring. She gives this kind of sleepy vibe to all of us. When I turned my head around to look at the back of the class, there were like five people asleep on their desks. She talked to fast that even my brain could not interpret it, so it kind of just shut itself down. Even Light can't take it. I enjoyed as I watched him trying to stay awake. See what I mean, it's so boring that the only source of entertainment was seeing Light trying to stay awake.

Suddenly a knock on the door came, it was Jean. Jean entered and asked to return Light's book. Jean does not take English Literature with us, it took me long enough to realize why. Light excuses himself and went out. I leaned my head on the desk and looked outside. The trees and grass were so soothing that I could fall asleep and the only thing separating me and the outside world is this window.

As I blinked, I was shocked so shocked that I could scream. There were words written in blood on the glass. It says "YOU DON'T BELONG HERE".

When I saw it, I accidentally kicked the desk, hurting my leg but I controlled the pain from it. It was written in blood, my inner voice was screaming loudly as my eyes were wide open. I tried to calm myself down, I have a feeling that it was my imagination, I took a deep breath and then blinked again. Sure enough, it disappeared. What was that? What is wrong with me? Am I losing my mind? I stayed calm as these thoughts came across my mind. Suddenly, my thoughts were disrupted as my smartphone vibrated in my pocket. I picked it up and it was a message from Danielle Fond who was just sitting behind me. She must have noticed my reaction. Danielle is another one of my close friends. Danielle has long brown hair and bright brown eyes. She wears a black skinny jeans with a brown sweater. Basically she is fashionable and she makes sure that everything matches. Danielle is rich, that's why she doesn't ride in the bus with most of us. She is a bit snobbish but that's a part of her. I forgot to mention something, Jean and Danielle are almost the same yet so far. Jean is the life of the party and Danielle is the spice of the party in a way too. She literally hook up with some random guys at a party, she is filled with a bit of lust. I don't care what my friends do because at the end of the day we are all still teenagers filled with hormones and all. We all know each other pretty well so there are no secrets kept between us. The only innocent ones I know are Jean and Light, so far because they are the smart ones but when it comes to English literature, Danielle beat them without a blink. Danielle is very good at English Literature, she won two awards for that. Danielle, Light and Jean are my best friends, I can't imagine life without them. They are part of me that I never want to change. The four of us hang out most of our time together. If I could change any of my friends personality, I wouldn't because that's why I choose them to be my friends. I cherish them. I took up my phone and replied Danielle's message.

DANIELLE: Hey, are you okay Max? MAXIEL : Of course, I am alright. Why wouldn't I be? DANIELLE: WOW, you are really bad in lying, even in the text I could sense the lie, spill it Greene.

MAXIEL: UGHH... Fine, I am just sleepy and I hallucinate something just now about something scary.

DANIELLE: HMM...scary huh? HAHAHA I never knew that Max who is also known as one of the best football players is afraid about something. BTW what did you hallucinate about?

MAXIEL: Just some BLOODY messages written on the window stating "YOU DON'T BELONG HERE".

DANIELLE: OOOHHHH SPOOKY, For a second there I thought you were just imagining about hot girls in bikini, that's why you got a boner and accidentally kicked the desk.

MAXIEL: DANIELLE WTFFF!!!, WHY WOULD YOU EVEN THINK OF THAT????

DANIELLE: Don't play innocent Greene, I know you have used it before;]

MAXIEL: I am ignoring you now.

DANIELLE: Fine, don't think too much about the hallucinations that you just had, you must be tired.

MAXIEL: Thanks, I think so too. Even Light told me that too.

DANIELLE: No problem if you need me just tell me because I am just right behind you since there are no other nicer nor hygienic places to sit.

MAXIEL: HAHAHA, YOU REALLY KNOW HOW TO LIGHT UP MY WORLD DANIELLE :)

DANIELLE: HUH, isn't that Light's job. I,

CHAPTER 3

UNFORGIVEN PAST

RECESS FINALLY!!!. The moment everyone was waiting for. I went to the cafeteria together with Danielle and Jean. After we collected our food fromfthe lady who was wearing a hairnet and a white shirt, we head towards our table.

That particular table was our spot and no one else; it was always facing a window where we could see a big oak tree. Danielle sat facing Jean and I sat facing opposite Light.

At that moment, I was staring at the burger filled with tomatoes and lettuce that I hoped it was. There's a box of milk and an apple beside it. "SO how are things, why do you seem a bit weird today?" Danielle questioned me.

"What do you mean by that" I replied. "Don't play dumb Greene, you know something that we don't" Danielle insisted of me telling her. "Fine the truth is I also don't really know what I am facing right now, I need time to think. I will inform you once I figure it out okay" I replied her but I did not make any eye contact, I was just staring at my tray of food. Light knew that something was disturbing me so he changed the topic. "By the way are you guys going to the party".

"Hell yeah, I need to be there" Danielle replied excitedly.

Jean looked at me in a concern way but she knew that I wouldn't want to talk about it. I could see that they wanted to question me about some things but they knew that I would be more disturbed about it.

That's why I love them, they understood me. They continued chatting about the party and how Danielle planned to show up in a tight dress or how Jean wants to help Elle to set up the party.

"Are you coming Max?" Jean asked me, while making eye contact.

"YOU NEED IT MAX" Light insisted.

"Yeah, all the football players are going to be there and I need someone hot to accompany me so that they don't make any moves on me" Danielle said with a smirk.

I looked at them, they look worried about me. Maybe I should go, at least to make them think that I am okay. I smiled at them and said "Yeah, I will come but on one condition, we go together".

"ALRIGHT, yes the party is going to be epic" Light cheered. Just two more subjects and then it is football practice. The bell then rang indicating that recess is over.

I have HISTORY next. Our HISTORY teacher is Mr. Mat Danerson. He likes the concept on how history effects the present. I really don't get the concept and idea of history. I mean why do we even have to study about dead people. I ask this to Mr. Mat and he said that we learn it so HISTORY doesn't repeat itself such as wars, revenge and so on. This is the 21 st century with technology rapidly evolving, I doubt that my generation will want to create war. I think that we would rather sleep and be on social media than creating war. If my generation decided to go for war, I have a feeling the war is going to be on a social media platform or a gaming competition but then again anything is possible. After History is Physics, in my opinion physics is boring so I am going to skip the details. Yes, why is today such a long day.

FOOTBALL PRACTICE FINALLY!!!. I love football since it helps me not to overthink stuff. I kind of have a rival that I like to go against, his name is DAMIAN MAINS. He is a bully. I walked towards the field with Light and Danielle. They accompanied me sometimes just to watch the progress of the practice. As I walked down I heard Danielle yelling "Yeah you go HOT STUFF, show them who you are". I instantly blushed. Why Danielle, why? Everyone started looking at me while I headed towards the locker room to change. In the locker room, guess who I met, up it was DAMIAN. DAMIAN looked at me and greeted me with a smirk "GOOD LUCK out there Greene". I was astonished. He normally just hit me on the shoulder or rolls up his eyes at me but why is he greeting me like that. As he was changing I asked him "What's your game, what are you planning". As he removes his shirt "Nothing I am just wishing you luck that's all", he replied innocently. He then put his hand up to shake my hand but I ignored it and pushed it away. "I am going to kick your ass on the field". He looked surprised when I said that, and then he looked up to me with a smirk "Well I will be looking forward to that". Okay, I know I am rude but that isn't Damian, that must be some kind of demon in there changing his attitude, Damian is a popular kid in our school just because he is rich and good looking. He has this brown spiky hair and blue iris eyes, that's all but for some reason all the girls go crazy for him. He is always so snobbish and he likes to brag about stuff a lot. The reason I don't like him a lot is because he once hurt Jean by spreading false rumors about her.

I ignored him and headed out to the field, I noticed something odd about the weather. Something about the weather today just put a smile on my face.

I love the weather, it seems like a nice day to play. It wasn't sunny or raining, it was just cloudy and nice.

"COME ON GUYS, GET ON THE FIELD" COACH Langford yelled. He is one of the greatest football strategist that I have known.

We played the first round and it was okay. The second round was going well until Damian tackled me hard. It was painful but luckily I managed to stabilize myself and not fall. I went to the corner taking off my head gear and started to pant. That pain, it feels weird as though electric currents went through me. Coach Langford stopped the game, Damian started approaching me.

"SO THAT WAS WHAT YOU WERE UP TO, IT WAS ON PURPOSE WASN'T IT" I yelled at the top of my lungs in anger towards him.

"No it wasn't honest, it was an accident" he looked guilty with his head lowered down. I ignored him.

"OKAY THAT'S ALL FOR TODAY, NICE WORK GUYS" coach Langford yelled.

I quickly went to the locker room and took a quick shower. Damian tried to talk to me in the showers, but I ignored him, cause I know he is planning something suspicious and also it was awkward, no one talks in the locker room. As I exited the locker room, I saw Jean joining Danielle and Light. I headed towards them. "Max I think you are being a bit rough on DAMIAN, who knows maybe he has changed" Light told me.

"I have a feeling something is wrong, something isn't right" I told them.

"WELL, sorry I am late anyway I had to help Mr Gilmert with something" Jean apologized.

"No problem, it wasn't such a great match either" I said.

Danielle looked sleepy though. I suggested let's head home. It was already 5 pm and we had to catch the bus home. We all headed towards the school bus stop. We started little conversations like how Mr Gilmer was, boring in Physics. Danielle then started to go on about some guy that she is thinking of nailing. Wow! that girl could go on for days. As we were walking, I tilted my head a little and guess who was in the woods, it was that girl in the white dress. What is she doing here and why is she wearing a dress in this cold cloudy weather. She does look adorable in that dress; it matches her pale skin. I stammered a bit when I was talking with them. I saw her smirking and waving at me. I know what I should do now. I need answers. I immediately left the group and chased after her. As she saw me running towards her, she moved towards the woods. The distance between us is a bit far, but I couldn't care less, I really need to know who is she? "W…WAI…WAIT" I yelled at her while running. As I entered into the woods, I tried to find her but I could not. There were a lot of trees blocking the pathway. The woods was a bit misty but it was still clear to see the surroundings. I tried to look around me to search for the girl but she just vanished out of thin air. How did she do that? "WHERE ARE YOU??" I yelled but there was no reply as though she was a ghost. "WHO ARE YOU AND WHAT DO YOU WANT FROM ME" I yelled again at the top of my lungs but there wasn't any reply. I looked confused at the same time I started panting to pay off my oxygen debt. I think I might and pushed my limit by running, especially with the heavy back pack that I am carrying. As I looked around trying to find the girl but there was nothing, it is like she had just vanished or evaporated out of nothing. I kept on looking and then suddenly a hand tapped on my back. "G…GAHH" I yelled in shock as I fell onto the ground. It was Light, I guess he had chased after me. He was panting harder than me. I guess he must have chased after me when he saw me taking off. I waited for a while until he caught his breath. We made eye contact and then suddenly he yelled out while panting "DUDE WHERE THE HELL YOU THINK YOU ARE GOING, YOU MADE US WORRIED". At that moment my head was filled with thoughts like who was that teenage girl? and where is she?.

"Don't do that again, don't you remember STACY'S CASE" he panted out. Stacy's case was a murder case. Last year a teenage girl was murdered in these woods. That was why our parents don't allow us to enter into these woods. The police had to close the case since there was no lead on it and it was taking so long so they put it as an accident. I saw her body, it was filled with blood as though someone had taken a hard rock and hit her head. I was close to her since she was my senior that time. Everyone knew it was a murder case but the police chose to put it as an accident since there was no lead.

"I am sorry, I saw the same girl in a white dress and I need to see who she was, that's why I ran towards her" I told Light as I was still laying on the ground.

Light held up his hand in order to help me up. I grabbed his hand as he pulled me up on my feet. "Don't ever do that again, you got us worried over nothing. Come on let's head back to Jean and Danielle, they must be worried. As we exited the woods, I heard a high pitch voice inside the woods but I chose to ignore it because I don't want to worry my friends anymore. As we exited the woods I saw Jean waving at us.

We went back to them. I explained about what I saw in the woods and the reason why I rushed towards the woods.

"OOOOO… spooky it could be a ghost you know" Danielle joked around. Jean looked up towards Danielle and shook her head in disagreement.

"Do you know who she was in case she really was a ghost" Jean asked me.

"Nope, I really had no idea who she was but for some reason she kept on smirking and waving at me as though she knew me.

"It could be STACY you know, I mean that is where she got murdered anyway" Danielle joked around again.

I knew that wasn't true because that girl looked completely different from Stacy. Stacy had brunette hair and a tan skin with deep light blue iris eyes but this girl was blonde and has a pale skin with bright yellow iris eyes. "Hahaha very funny Danielle, no that couldn't be, cause this girl is completely different compared to Stacy" I said to them. I think Danielle was thinking about that, because she had watched to many movies and read too many books. I guess this is why her mind is so creative and isn't as close to the point of reality. As we were chatting while walking, a sports car pulled over. It was Danielle's driver. Remember the part where I said Danielle was rich, yes she isn't rich. She is crazy rich. Richer than Damian the bully.

"Anyway my ride has come, by the way do you guys want a ride home?" Danielle asked us. We rejected the idea politely because we prefer to take the bus and we don't really want to trouble Danielle's driver. I looked at Jean and Light as we headed towards the bus stop. Thank God we are far away from the woods cause it would just trouble my mind and make me overthink.

"So do you want to talk about the imaginary girl who you were chasing about earlier?" Jean asked me politely.

I want to talk about it but then again I don't want to make them worried. "Neh… it is okay, I was probably just to sleepy that is why I was hallucinating" I replied Jean.

"Yap! that must be the problem cause I mean a girl in white dress in this cold weather, it seems illogical" Light interrupted.

Jean shook her head as we have reached the bus stop.

CHAPTER 4

SHALLOW LIGHT

We all have that one secret where we want to tell someone but we couldn't because behind every smile lies something dark.

Basically we are trying to avoid making things awkward.

As for today, Light was staying over at my house. I asked him to do so because I really need him to tutor me for chemistry since I am falling behind class. I headed to my house and pulled out a pair of keys that I kept inside the bag. I put the keys in the door and unlocked it.

"I am sorry for troubling you on this but I really need your help in order to pass the chemistry test" I sighed.

Light tilted his head "OH…come on don't be like that, what are friends for anyway and also I really want to enter your house for the first time without using the windows" Light smirked.

"You sure, cause it seems like I am really troubling you for this" I sighed again.

"Dude seriously no problem, you seriously got to chill, this is also beneficial for me since I could revise the subject for myself", Light replied.

I actually overheard him making plans to go out for dinner with someone tonight so I kind of feel bad for ruining his plans.

As we entered, I inform him that dinner won't be arriving until 7:30.

"If dinner is at 7:30 then why don't we study first, then maybe after dinner we could watch a horror film or something", Light suggested.

I nodded towards Light's idea in agreement. We headed upstairs and I brought him into my room and pulled out the chemistry book in my drawer. Light then tutored me until 7:20. Light is perfect for teaching me this subject and he is really patient with me even though I kept on scratching my head on the subject. At 7:20 we headed downstairs to watch television while waiting for dinner to arrive. My mom was a bit late as she arrived with the fast food at 7:45. We ate our dinner while having some small talk with my mom such as HOW WAS SCHOOL? and basically that's what all we talked about. My mom was thrilled when she found out that Light was tutoring me in chemistry, I sighed as I heard the subject chemistry. We all have that one subject that could question our life decisions and what the HELL are we doing with our life. For me that was chemistry. After dinner we headed to the hall.

"Hey Max, why were you rough with Damian during football practice" Light asked.

I was shocked as he asked about Damian.

"Why wouldn't I be? He did hit me but luckily I caught my balance. You knew how he treated me two years ago and some other kids. He was a bully, he would sometimes tease us and beat us up" I replied in frustrations.

"That was two years ago, come on, people change. Don't you think you should let go of it?" I shook my head in disagreement.

"Light why are you on his side anyway. Aren't you my friend, why are you siding that bully anyway" I questioned Light suspiciously.

"He isn't a bully and I am not siding anyone, I just think that you should give up this silly rivalry between you two. You might not know this but I think he is trying to make amends with you, why not forgive him and just move on?" I lifted my left eyebrows out in confusion.

Why is Light siding Damian. Light is good with PSYCHOLOGY maybe he saw something different in Damian. Am I wrong? Was I really wrong to yell at Damian earlier? NO I AM NOT, HE DESERVES IT. My subconscious yelled at me. Light tilted his head looking confused as he knew that I was overthinking with thoughts in my head. "UGHH… forget about it, so what movie do you want to watch?" Light asked me. I then let go of my thoughts as I pulled out a horror movie out of the drawer underneath the television. I showed it to Light and he nodded in agreement. He nodded in a weird way as in like he was a bit frustrated and sad. Was it something I said? DAMN IT, I am overthinking again, what is wrong with me?. I am not usually like this. This all started happening after that weird dream. I ignored Light's feelings and emotions that time as I put in the movie into the video player. We watched the movie for a couple of minutes and I started dozing off. I stopped dozing off as I was surprised when a voice yelled out loud YOU DON'T BELONG HERE. I quickly averted my head to find the source of the sound and it was the television. DAMN IT GET A HOLD OF YOURSELF MAX, I yelled at myself in thought. Light excuses himself to the restroom. It was only me in the hall, my mom was fast asleep in her room, she must be tired. I looked at the direction of the clock as it pointed to the time 10:21 p.m. I suddenly heard a buzzing on the table. It was Light's phone. Hmm…

he isn't here for the moment so I quickly took a peak on his phone and it completely shocked me. My jaw dropped in shock and confusion. It all make perfect sense now, why didn't I realize it earlier? WHY didn't Light tell me about this? A lot of questions were on my head until I heard Light entered the hallway. He saw me holding his phone and he grabbed it out of my hand.

"YOU SHOULDN'T DO THAT TO PEOPLE'S PHONE YOU KNOW" he scolded me.

I didn't reply him because my jaw was still on the ground as I couldn't believe what I just read.

"Helloo… are you okay dude" Light waved his hand in front of my face.

Then he looked at his phone and he was shocked. He now knew that I know his secret but he wasn't panicking as he was just as still as a rock. I still can't believe I saw that message. It was from JEAN and it stated "SINCE YOU CANCELED OUR DATE TODAY, LET'S GO OUT ON THURSDAY OKAY?". Light is dating Jean, this explains a lot now. "So now you know huh?" Light smirked. I turned to Light in shock.

"W…wh…why didn't you tell me?" I questioned.

Light tilted his head and still has that smirk on his face. Isn't he scared that I now know his secret? He seemed so confident with himself.

"You kind off going through some stuff right now remember?".

I managed to get a hold of myself by taking a couple of deep breaths.

"Aren't you afraid that I now know your secret about you and Jean" I questioned Light with a smirk.

"Hmm…not really cause the whole school knows about it. Everyone knows including Danielle. Only you and my folks don't know about it" Light smirked.

"Say what now, why am I the only one who doesn't know about this and why don't I see you guys hanging out or making out in front of me?" I questioned Light in anger.

Light looked at me puzzled.

"Do you want me to make out with Jean in front of you and Danielle?" Light questioned me with a smirk.

"No, that isn't what I meant, I mean isn't that what people normally do and why was I the last one to know? I questioned Light.

"Dude why do you think I hang out with Jean most of the time, I am with you. Of course you might have thought that we were only friends but that isn't the case right now though. Even the whole school is not acting up as you do. It is the 21st century remember, this is kind of normal for teenagers like us" Light explained.

He took his phone and replied to Jean in front of me.

LIGHT: Sorry for the cancelations Jean.

After that text he immediately got a reply from Jean. It wasn't even a second.

JEAN: Don't worry about it. Maxiel is our friend, you should help him in his studies.

LIGHT : OHHH… and yes I am free on Saturday. BTW Maxiel found out about us.

JEAN: Wait what? Really? What did he say???

LIGHT: He doesn't mind it.

"I didn't say that" I said to Light after Light sent that message. "Dude you are my friend not my mom or wutt" Light replied.

JEAN: Well that was unexpected, I felt really bad for not telling him about us sooner.

LIGHT: He forgives us, just be nice to him starting from now onwards okay and don't make it awkward.

JEAN: Okay:]

JEAN: BTW, need to go now, love you Light

LIGHT: Right back at you.

Light was surprisingly happy, I didn't realize this. I thought I was supposed to be mad cause he is dating one of my best friends but then again who am I to control him? It is his life, he could do whatever he want with it. In a way, I am kind of happy for them. I started laughing out loud. Light was completely shocked by my reaction.

"Are you okay or are you still in shock about it" Light questioned.

"NO I am not, yes I am surprised but then again you guys are my friends and I am happy for the both of you" I replied.

Light then just smiled at me in happiness. He looked as though a huge burden had just been lifted up of his shoulders.

Today was really interesting and unexpected, I thought to myself. After we settled that, we went back watching that cheesy horror movie. After watching the movie halfway, we kind of felt sleepy and then we decided to go to bed. It was 15 minutes to twelve. We went and brushed our teeth before bedtime. While Light was brushing his teeth I was just smiling to myself looking back at today. After he came out, I pulled out a mattress and set it up for him. I then jumped onto my bed and switched off the lamp, now it was just me in the darkness staring at the ceiling. The air was cool as it was from the air conditioning. It started to drizzle a bit outside. My head was clouded with thoughts again like who was that girl in the white dress? Then a voice came and broke my chain of thoughts.

"Hey Max, now that you know that I am dating Jean does it affect your opinion about me" Light asked.

"Light you have always been my friend. You have helped me in more times than I could ever remember. It just doesn't change our friendship. I still like you and Jean both. I mean yeah sure it was surprising and shocking at the beginning, I was also a bit disappointed that you did not tell me about Jean" I sighed. I started hearing Light laughing and was wandering what was it about. It was now raining heavily I love this feeling, the feeling of rain, when it rains heavily outside and I am just underneath this warm and cozy blanket. The difference in temperature between outside and inside is what that comforts me.

"I didn't expect you to be so understanding in that short amount of time though. I thought it was going to be weird and all" Light sighed in relief.

"I couldn't be mad at you, after all you have done so many things in my life that brought me to this moment. Jean and Danielle too have done that and that is why I like you guys so it's hard for me to be mad at you guys" I replied.

Now there were thunder and lightning. I left the window beside me open because I felt more comfortable with it. I could see the branch and leaves getting wet outside.

"Well thanks Max for understanding the situation, anyway GOODNIGHT I am really sleepy" Light yawned.

"Goodnight Light" I replied.

For some reason I kind of felt a feeling of relief in my mind and I was a bit happy as though someone has helped me carry my luggage of troubles. I just love this feeling right now, my heart is filled with warmth and comfort. At this point, I had forgotten the troubles that I am facing.

As I looked out the window I was shocked as I saw the girl in white dress sitting on top of the tree branch looking at me but this time she wasn't smiling or waving, she was just staring at me with a scary look on her face. I then pulled up my blanket and ignored it. As I blinked I thought to myself, is she gone? I took a peek and saw the same type of horror again as I saw the words YOU DON'T BELONG HERE, GET OUT. I was completely scared that even words for help couldn't even escape my throat. That girl in the white dress disappeared, the only thing that I saw was that horrifying words that is now imprinted on my mind. I then managed to gather up my courage and switched on the lamp.

As I turned on the room light, those words completely vanished. Now my room was filled with Light instead of darkness. What kind of sick prank is that? I thought to myself. Light then started mumbling as the brightness woke him up.

"HUHHHH... WHY DID YOU SWITCH ON THE LAMP, IS EVERYTHING OKAY?" Light mumbled out loud.

I did not reply as I was still confused and puzzled about the situation earlier. What is going on? I started panting as my heartbeat increased rapidly while my head was overflowing with thoughts and fear. Suddenly, someone tapped on my shoulder that startled me. It was Light. He was standing in front of me while only wearing his black boxers and socks. There was a cross hanging from his neck to his chest. Huh... I have never seen that cross before, it was black with white corners. I was just sitting on top of my bed with my legs folded. "You okay" he asked. I manage to get a grip of myself.

"SORRY, IT WAS JUST A NIGHTMARE" I replied while still trying to calm myself down. Light knew that was a LIE.

"You got to tell me what is going on, if not I couldn't help you" Light sighed out in worry.

I looked at him and then explained everything. I knew if I didn't tell him, he wouldn't let me off the hook until I told the TRUTH. I explained every single detail about the girl in the white dress and that weird message that I couldn't stop seeing everywhere. It was still raining heavily and I looked at the clock it showed the time 10:21 again. It couldn't be, the time must have been busted. I reached out on my phone that was on my desk in front of my bed and checked the time and it was 2.45a.m. I couldn't believe it was already 2.45a.m. that was quick. Light thought to himself for a while and then reached out to the binds beside me and pulled it down. He blocked the outside view.

"You are either seeing it or you are probably hallucinating. If you are seeing it for real then I couldn't help you but too call the police and inform that there was an intruder on your property. If you are hallucinating then it is probably that your subconscious is trying to tell you or even warn you about something" Light explained.

"Thanks Light, that made me feel better, maybe I am just tired" I sighed anxiously.

"For now I suggest that you go to bed and we will talk about it first thing in the morning cause it is still kind of early for your brain to function"

Light said. I laughed slightly as he tried to make me feel better. He then switched off the lamp.

"Try going to sleep for now, if you couldn't fall asleep in half and hour, wake me up. We could watch a movie and then prepare for school" Light yawned.

That made me feel better a bit, but why is this all happening to me? The rain suddenly stopped as I couldn't hear any raindrops outside. As I was thinking to myself, my eyes suddenly felt heavy and then everything went pitch black. When everything went pitch black, I remembered something that had happened sometime ago in school. It was Jean, she was crying about something. I tried to talk to her but she avoided me at the school playground. She headed up in front of the school porch and sat down on the swing there trying to control her tears from flowing. I followed her and I watched.

A few seconds later Light came. He knelt on one of his knee and started talking to Jean about something. I never knew an optimist like Jean could cry like that.

I could only Jean's lips moving but I couldn't hear what was actually going on. They seem to be talking about something. If only I could hear them

Suddenly, Light then pulled her head closer and kissed her.

After their lips separated, Jean looked surprised by that. It started to become blurry to me suddenly. Why am I remembering this now? What does this mean? Is this how they got together? A flood of thoughts overflowed my head as everything went pitch black. I felt incredibly weak now as though I couldn't even make a single move. It was just me and this darkness that surrounds me. I heard a loud voice saying to me "It is okay, it will all be over soon". Who was that? I thought to myself before my eyes felt heavy and closed on its' own.

CHAPTER 5

LIVING DREAMS

BEEP BEEP BEEP. It was my alarm clock. My mind told me to wake up but my body says no. I am really tired, do I really have to go to school today?

I suddenly felt something as though someone shook my body, it was Light. "It is time to wake up now". He just kept on tapping and pulling me until I was awake.

He already got ready for school. He was wearing a long sleeve white T-shirt with black skinny jeans and socks. He folded his long sleeve, halfway, he likes doing that.

Gezz.. what time does he wakes up?

I can't believe that hee was already ready while I am still in my black long sleeve undershirt and blue boxers. I managed to gather all the energy inside of me to wake myself up.

I head towards the bathroom to shower while Light was helping my mom to prepare breakfast.

I usually shower with cold water to keep myself awake but I hated the feeling of that cold water touching my warm skin.

After I showered, I came out and took a blue shirt and a brown pair of pants. I headed down as breakfast was ready. It was pancakes.

After breakfast we headed to school, I hope today ends quickly.

As I arrived to school, time flew by quite fast. It seems as though my wish had come true. Everything was fine so far in class, nothing disturbed me till recess.

During recess, Light, Danielle, Jean and me headed to the big tree at our school. It was also one of our spots to hang out. We hung out there because we wanted to see some snowflakes. We had our jackets on so that we won't catch a cold. It was a beautiful moment that I cherished very much even though we had some stupid conversations. It seems like today was going to be okay after all.

After recess we headed back to our class. I thought today was going to be okay but then life always has its way of proving me wrong.

Our next subject was biology, this is when something weird happens.

During BIOLOGY, we learned about the human brain and how hallucinations were formed. Our brain hallucinates when we are on something like drugs or alcohol. This means that I wasn't really hallucinating, I was seeing something real all this while. Knowing this truly disturbs me. I picked up my phone and started texting Light. He was sitting two rows behind me and his seat was also beside the window like mine.

MAXIEL: If Miss Jade is telling the truth about hallucinations then I might be in trouble.

I instantly got a message from Light after that, it means that I am not the only one who isn't paying any attention in class.

LIGHT: Why? What do you mean by that?

MAXIEL: Miss Jade says that hallucination could only occur when we are high which is consuming alcohol or by taking drugs. Then it means that I wasn't hallucinating all this while.

Danielle was beside me and she started to peek over to who I was texting. She was just staring at the messages that Light and me were exchanging. I ignored her as I was more concerned about what I am facing.

LIGHT: I thought I didn't have to tell you this but you weren't hallucinating. I knew it all along. Your body language says that you are speaking the truth.

MAXIEL: WAIT WHATTTTTT? WHY DIDN'T YOU TELL ME THIS??

As I was texting, I suddenly heard a loud voice calling out my name. "MR.GREENE IF YOU DON'T WANT TO PAY ATTENTION IN CLASS THEN WHY ARE YOU EVEN HERE?" It was from Miss Jade.

That loud voice of hers shocked all of us including Danielle who was beside me as I saw her tremble a bit. Miss Jade looked mad, damn I am screwed right now.

"Let's see who you are busy texting right now" Miss Jade asked.

Now since I know the situation that I am facing and I don't want to cause Light any trouble. With my quick thinking, I quickly came out of the chat with Light. I then straight away went to the internet and searched about the brain functions. I did that all while making eye contact with Miss Jade. I managed to memorize each letter positions on the key pad so I know what I was doing. It only took me ten seconds to do so.

I then handed my phone to Miss Jade. When she saw what I was doing, she handed back my phone.

"Impressive Maxiel, sorry I doubted you. I didn't know you were doing some research on your own" Miss Jade's tone was calm and happy.

I turned over to Light and nodded indicating that we manage to dodge that bullet. Light looked puzzled as if he was expecting another reaction from Miss Jade. I never expected that I would see Light confused, this is new for me.

LIGHT: How did you do that?

Maxiel: We shall continue our talk later as I am afraid that I might get caught again. You know how sharp Miss Jade senses are. We are just lucky that we manage to dodge detention.

LIGHT: Well done, impressive. We shall continue our talk later, until then don't worry or overthink too much of your situation okay. Thanks also for helping me dodge that.

MAXIEL: I don't want to cause you detention, it is my fault anyway for bringing this out in class.

I then placed my phone back into my pocket but there was a sudden vibration in my pocket, it must be Light what is he saying now? I told him later right? I took out my phone and just went through a quick glance.

LIGHT: Meet me after school the bleachers near the football field

Maxiel: Okay, got it.

I quickly put back my phone into my pocket and start listening to Miss Jade's lectures. Danielle leaned closer to me and then whispered in my year "Quick thinking there Greene, bet you can't pull it off next time". I just turned to Danielle facing her dark blue eyes and just smirked at her.

After school, I headed over to the bleachers to meet Light. Danielle followed me as she was curious about what Light and me wanted to discuss about. I tried stopping her but she wouldn't let it go. She followed me to the bleachers. Light and Jean were there. My guess is that Jean was curious about the same thing as Danielle is too. We headed over to them and Light asked" You okay?". "To be honest, I think I am okay. I didn't see anything today. So it must be over" I replied.

"WHY? WHAT IS HAPPENING?" Danielle asked curiously.

"I was just seeing things but it is over now, I hope" I replied.

"Let's keep it that way, Danielle let's not talk about it" Light told Danielle politely.

"Okay if you say so, instead can we talk about Elle's party this weekend?" Danielle asked excitedly.

Hmmm… I almost forgot about that. I started smiling to myself and just thinking of the fun that we will have during that party. I am sure it would be fun for all of us. It is going to be my first high school party, I really can't wait for it "Maxiel are you sure you are okay? Stop smiling to yourself, you are creeping me out" Jean laughed out.

"He must be having perverted thoughts right now" Light smirked.

"Wha… What, N…No I am not" I replied anxiously.

"OH OHH… he is replying anxiously meaning its true" Danielle joked.

I started blushing as those thoughts of what they said imprinted on my head.

"Relax, you are a jock. You are supposed to have fun with girls like me, you know entertain us with the stuff" Danielle bit her lower lip in lust.

I started to laugh as Danielle bit her lower lip.

"Seriously why are you laughing? This is my sexy face, can't you see it? Is it that bad?" Danielle asked.

I couldn't control my laughter. When I was laughing, I noticed those smiles on their face as though they were happy and glad that I started showing them my happiness.

"Thanks Danielle, I really appreciate it. Only you could light up my world" I smirked.

"Again that is Light's job, how many times must I tell you that Danielle and I light up people's world. I leaned closer to Danielle and gave her a kiss on the cheek indicating that I appreciated her. Light and Jean were completely shocked with what I did.

"Gezz.. what was that for?" Danielle asked.

"A THANK YOU SIGN" I replied.

"What are you, my grandfather? You owe me one for making your day Max" Danielle rolled her eyes while smirking.

"Anyway Jean I picked up a perfect outfit for you for the party, don't come in looking like that" Danielle pointed at Jean's clothes. Jean instantly rolled up her eyes.

"What's wrong with this outfit" Jean asked Danielle.

"Nothing, it is just so you and common, which is a bad thing" Danielle replied.

Jean kept on denying Danielle's offer until she finally gave in.

"Okay but make sure the outfit is prefect okay" Jean stated.

"BITCH, you are talking to Danielle here" Danielle flipped her hair while saying that. The three of us started to laugh.

"Gosh, I need friends who understands me" Danielle stated.

Light, Jean and I looked at each other. Then we hugged Danielle tightly. She was shocked with what we did. "But I will just settle with you guys" Danielle giggled a bit. The four of us walked home together, during that time I have forgotten everything, I was just listening to the voice inside my head that asked me to appreciate this time and cherish it to the depth of my heart. I was happy. Danielle got into her car with the driver in front and we waved her off. The smile on her face was so genuine and honest. The three of us walked home and I separated from Light and Jean. I gave them the privacy that they needed. I don't want to be the third wheel that time. I headed towards the bus stop and while heading there, I couldn't wipe of the smile on my face. Everything was perfect, I wished this moment could last forever.

Throughout my journey from school to home, I just can't shake off the feeling of happiness. I reached home a bit late since there weren't any bus around but it was okay I don't mind. When I reached home, my mom was there with dinner on the table.

"Oh honey, you looked happy. Anything interesting happened today" my mom smiled.

I nodded my head and headed upstairs to take a shower.

During dinner, I had small talks with my mom and I told her about my day. It was such a bright day for me. I head to bed early cause I can't wait for school tomorrow. As I went to bed thinking of all the happiness I had and how grateful I am to have friends like them. My heart was filled with warmth. As my thoughts were running with happiness my eyes suddenly felt heavy. I shut my eyes and imagined the people that I love. I suddenly woke up in darkness, it was dark. All I could see was trees and then what I saw horrified me. There are three corpses in front of me. As I move closer to them, it shocked me as tears started rolling down my face "NO…NO… PLEASE DON'T LEAVE ME" I stammered. Those corpses were my three beloved friends. It was Light, Jean and Danielle. Suddenly, something in white just crossed in front of me. It was the girl in white dress, she was holding a gun in her hand and it was filled with blood. This time she was wearing a mask, a white skull mask. "YOU DID THIS DIDN'T YOU" I was filled with anger she suddenly disappeared in front of me.

Out of nowhere she appeared and pushed me from behind and I slipped into the woods. I hit my head on a branch and then I woke up and brightness hit me. There was an irritating sound of BEEP'S from my alarm clock.

As I woke up, I started to pant really hard as though I had ran for hours. I managed to get a grip of reality and figured out that it was just a dream. It was an awful dream.

I looked at the clock at it was six in the morning, it is time to go to school. I did my usual routine and went down to have breakfast with my mom. I closed the door behind me as the school bus had arrived in front of my porch and started to honk.

I felt weird that moment but I chose to ignore it. I have a feeling that all my worries will be gone as soon as I see Light, Danielle and Jean. Right now only their smiles could make everything feel better. As I got to school, I accidentally bumped into Damian. "Hey MAXIEL, I need to talk to you". I ignored him and went to our classroom. As I entered the classroom, I saw the three of them laughing and chatting together.

"Hey Max, come on join us. Danielle is showing us a picture of her Halloween costume last year" Light invited me.

I sat down on the chair beside Light and was now facing Danielle. I looked outside the window, the sky turn cloudy and it was starting to drizzle. We were just chatting while waiting for Mr Gilmert, our physics teacher. Danielle then showed me the picture that she mentioned, she went as a sexy and creepy nurse clown. Wow! I did not expect I will be using nurse and clown together as one thing. The class was starting to get noisy as the sky was roaring with thunder and lightning. It started to rain heavily it was truly a beautiful view. After a couple of minutes, Mr Gilmert arrived.

"SORRY, class I had to speak with Mr Adams our principal about something", Mr Gilmert stated. Light, Danielle, Jean and I had a group chat that we talked about if there is something important. My phone started to vibrate after a few minutes. It was a text from Danielle.

DANIELLE: Guys, I forgot to tell you this, but this Sunday my family is having a charity ball and you guys are invited.

LIGHT: What about ELLE'S party?

DANIELLE: Her party is on Friday night, mine is on Saturday night.

JEAN: What is the charity for?

DANIELLE: The environment sweetheart...;]

MAXIEL: Seems fun, okay I am coming.

DANIELLE: Great you will be my date for the night.

LIGHT: I can't confirm right now but I will tell you soon okay.

JEAN: Yeah me too.

DANIELLE: OKAY, but I do hope you guys do make it.

MAXIEL: Let's talk during recess okay:]

DANIELLE: NO take backs Maxiel.

I thought to myself, I agree to go to the ball because I want to have an in view of Danielle's house since we have all never actually been in before.

CHAPTER 6

LIVE AND PARTY

During recess we met up at our usual place, the place that we imprinted on. Danielle starts to explain about our attire and then Light and I have to get a suit while Jean has to wear a beautiful dress since we are going to dine with high society.

She told us not to worry about the clothing since she got her own tailor and that we have to go there after school since it is going to be a rush.

"Since Maxiel is my date, I will fix you up with a suit. Light don't worry I will help you too with the suit. Finally, Jean, we are going shopping and then to the salon on Saturday morning. Once I fix you up, I guaranteed that Light couldn't keep his hands off you" Danielle explained.

Jean started to blush as her cheeks turned pinkish red. She also explained about the rules and how to behave. Being part of high society is tough, there are so many rules.

"So are you guys interested in coming to the ball?" Danielle asked.

Light, Jean and me looked at each other and shook our heads.

"Yes we will come but on one condition, you have to be with us on all time" Light explained.

"Deal but promise, me that you guys will behave and try not to embarrass me okay".

The three of us nodded at each other. Then after we talked about the ball we switch to ELLE'S party.

"Jean and I are helping ELLE with the party preparations, so Light and Maxiel you guys go to the mall after dealing with the tailor and get her a gift" Danielle ordered us. With all her plans in organizing us, she could definitely take the part of a leader one day. Her plan seems to have no flaws at all so far. I just hope everything goes as planned.

After school Light and I head towards the tailor Danielle told us to go. She gave us the address, it was 2199 EDINBURG STREET. When we reached to the tailor, we couldn't believe how fancy it was. I called up Danielle and told her that we could not afford it.

"You idiots, that is one of my dad's shop, so you guys don't have to pay for it, take it as a gift from me and I have already informed my dad about it so relax", Danielle explained.

I told Light about it as we entered into the tailor's shop.

There was a man in a suit, he has grey hair with PITCH BLACK eyes.

"Hah… yes do come in, I am guessing that you are Miss Danielle's friends?" the man in black suit asked us.

We nodded as he brought us to a room. The man brought us in one by one and measured our size. We have to strip down to our boxers since Danielle ordered slim fitting suits for us. As the man measured my waist, arm length and others, I asked Light a question who was currently waiting outside the room since he had already been measured.

"So what do we get one of the richest girl in our school for her birthday?" I asked.

"Something that she wouldn't have even though if she asked for it" Light replied.

"Wait, we are talking about materialistic stuff right, something that you could actually buy?" I questioned Light.

There was a slight pause for a moment and then I heard Light yelled out in excitement. "THAT'S IT". "Wait, what's, it?" I asked.

"Think about it she is rich and she is having a party. How many people will actually come to celebrate her birthday?" People are only coming there since there's alcohol and popular people. Meaning they wouldn't actually come to celebrate her birthday, they will come for the wrong reasons" Light explained.

"So what is this brilliant idea of yours?" I asked.

"Well since there is a huge space in her backyard, we will use that space and make our own small party for her" Light explained excitingly.

I'm still a bit puzzled so I just decided to go with it. After the appointment with the tailor, we headed to the mall and bought this small party stuff such as confetti, party hats and others. We even bought a small vanilla cake for Elle since that is her favorite.

We then called up Danielle and explained Light's idea to her. She surprisingly agreed to it. We asked her to stall Elle for the time when we are decorating the place.

Thank God Friday is a public holiday. We were all excited for it. I took the stuff we bought and store it in my house for two days including the cake.

Time passed quickly that time. We went to school as normal for the next two days and confirm with our plans.

FRIDAY has finally arrived, it is the day. Danielle told ELLE that we are going to help her with the decorations. Light and I carried the party stuff in our bag. Jean will then take the cake from my house when she is heading towards here.

When we arrived at Elle's, it took us a moment or two to look in disbelief on how big her house is. Elle opened up the gate as she welcomed us.

"Hey, thanks guys for helping with this stuff" Elle exclaimed.

She looked tired, maybe she was too excited with the party or she was too afraid that her parents would come home any moment soon. Danielle told us that Elle's parents went on a business trip last weekend and that they will only come home on Saturday night.

It was so convenient as though that was a sign for her to have this party. Elle then brought us into her house.

Danielle was waiting at the stairs and was just staring at us as Elle was explaining where the beer can, should be. It seems like ELLE is such a perfectionist. As Elle headed out to continue her preparations, Danielle approached us "I will handle the stuff with Elle right now, you guys do whatever you have to in the backyard".

We managed to sneak into Elle's backyard I guess Elle must be too tired to notice anything right now. We saw a couple of huge trees in her backyard that we used to our advantage. We use it to block the view so that nobody could notice anything. Danielle also informed that there was a generator in her store room. It was my job to sneak it into the backyard so when Elle wasn't looking, I broke into the store room and sneak out the generator.

Our plan so far is going quite well without any flaws. We managed to finish doing what we should at three in the afternoon and it was well hidden. I hope that Elle suddenly don't decide to come behind this trees to do anything.

Light and I were quite satisfied with our work. Now we just have to wait for everything to go according to plan. We went home around four in the afternoon after Danielle check out everything. Light and I then headed home together. We separated at the intersection. Danielle planned to stay there with Elle, she even brought spare clothes for the party.

As soon as I reached home I took a short nap because I know that tonight is going to be a long night. As I lay down on my bed, my eyelids felt heavy and they shut. I was calm.

BEEP! BEEP! BEEP! my alarm rings, I managed to force myself out of bed and switched it off. It was 6 p.m., the party starts at 8p.m. I went and took a quick shower. I chose to wear an orange shirt with a black hoodie and a pair of brown skinny jeans. After I was done I heard my mom calling me "Maxiel come on down, there are people waiting for you here. Who could that be? I mean seriously I wasn't expecting anyone this time. Some people meaning it was more than one right. I headed downstairs and I was shocked.

At the front door stood Light, Jean and Danielle.

"Hey I thought I was supposed to be meeting you guys there. Danielle didn't you bring spare clothes there" I asked.

"Remember we made a promise to go together with you to the party" Danielle's face palms herself.

"I MEAN, I DI...DIDN'T EXPECT YOU GUYS TO BE HERE", I stammered out loud with shock.

"Well like it or not we already made you a promise and since you are our friend we are bound by the promise no matter how much the trouble it will cause us" Jean says with a bright smile on her face.

"Tell me about it, my driver wasn't free so I had to use the bus to get here" Danielle rolled out her eyes while smiling at me.

"Come on we don't want to be late now do we?" Light was just smiling as his arms were around Jean.

At this moment I felt as though the world was rotating around me as my heart was filled with warmth only I could understand. I know how much trouble it takes to get here in a short time but they insisted on it just to keep a lousy promise that I wasn't even serious about it. I guess that is what makes them so special to me, they take everything too seriously.

We headed out taking the bus and we arrived at the party at 8.15p.m. It was noisy as we saw the football team drinking booze on the porch. Almost the whole school was there. As we entered into the house we managed to spot Elle.

"We will head on with our plan only at 9.15 p.m. okay, which is an hour from now" Danielle looked at us intimidatingly. We just nod our head agreeing to her.

One thing I know about Danielle is that she is good at pointing out the right time and location when there is an event. Hopefully everything just goes as planned right now.

"Until then you guys are free to do whatever you want to" Danielle said to us.

She separated from us and headed towards Elle and her friends. Elle was wearing something unusual, she was just wearing skinny jeans and a brown shirt with black top. Hmm! I did not expect her to be humble, I always thought that rich girls were snobbish but I was wrong as I met Danielle. She isn't that bad. I looked at ELLE and for some reason she doesn't seem to happy, maybe what Light said was true. Elle seemed like she was putting on a fake smile or a show for people.

Light and Jean separated from me as they told me that they need some privacy as they went off upstairs giggling. So now it was just me and this whole crowd of people. I headed outside to the backyard to just check on things. I walked forward as I set myself a distance from the party. On my way to the backyard, I bumped into someone I didn't expect too. It just had to be him of all people. It was Damian, he seemed pretty drunk. I tried to avoid him but he grabbed hold of my wrist while his other hand was holding a red plastic cup. My guess is that, it was filled with alcohol.

"Maxiel I need to talk to you" Damian said.

I tried to release my wrist from his hand but he was just too strong. As I tried to release myself, he slammed me into the tree that was behind me. His hand pinned both my wrists down and then the unexpected happen. He locked his lips with mine and forced his tongue into me.

Remember the part where I said that we all have that one deep and dark secret that we couldn't tell anyone even if we wanted too. Well apparently this was Damian's secret.

As he locked his lips upon mine, I blurred out for a while as my brain tries to process the information. I managed to get ahold of the situation and unpin myself from him. I then punched Damian on the face. He let go of me.

"DON'T EVER PULL THAT ON ME AGAIN" I yelled out in anger.

I looked at him and he seemed sad as for what he did to me. His brown eyes seemed cold as though he had done something that he didn't want to. I headed back to the party while leaving Damian on his knees.

As I head there, I checked on the time at it was 9.00p.m. Huh... time sure passed fast around here. My phone started to vibrate and it was a message from Danielle.

DANIELLE: Are you guys ready?

LIGHT: Just give us a minute to get our clothes on.

MAXIEL: EWWW... you don't have to tell us that.

JEAN: My thoughts exactly. Thanks Light for telling them

DANIELLE: How the hell are you guys doing it while texting?

LIGHT: OHH... we have our ways sweetheart.

JEAN: SHUT UP LIGHT!!!

MAXIEL: I am on my way there.

After three minutes

LIGHT: Okay, we are on our way there too.

DANIELLE: Jean where is the cake?

JEAN: I left it on the portable table that Light brought.

DANIELLE: Maxiel since you are going there now, I need you to switch on the generator.

MAXIEL: GOT IT!!! By the way how did you manage to convince Elle to go to the backyard.

DANIELLE: I got her drunk.

JEAN: SAY WHATTTT!!!

LIGHT: WHY DID YOU GET HER DRUNK?

DANIELLE: Yeah I am not good in convincing people and talking to them so this is the easiest way.

JEAN: How the HELL, are we going to celebrate now if she is drunk?

DANIELLE: Trust me, I know what I am doing. Plus if I ask her to come to the backyard, I have a feeling that she will ask a lot of questions.

MAXIEL: I have no idea what to say now.

As I reached at the backyard I saw the generator and turned it on, it was noisy but it was also worth it. The beautiful view of the bulbs lighting up the darkness is really a view to die for. I am proud of our work. We really arranged the bulbs nicely and made sure that it is aligned. I then took out the small vanilla cake. I took out one big candle and seven small candles to light it up. My phone then started to vibrate again.

DANIELLE: MAXIEL please also light up the candles for the cake.

MAXIEL: DONE.

As I typed in the message I saw two dark shadows heading towards the lighted area. It was Light and Jean. "Everything is going according to plan except ELLE is drunk" Jean stated. Our phones then begin to vibrate again, it was another message from Danielle.

DANIELLE: Okay I am bringing her over right now.

JEAN: Okay, we are all already here

We all got into our hiding positions. Jean and Light hid beside a tree while I chose to hide underneath the table.

As we all hid from the place, we can see two shadows heading towards us. As the shadows got closer and closer to the lighted area, all three of us jumped out and yelled out SURPRISE!!! Danielle seem to be helping Elle out with her balance, making sure that she doesn't actually fall down. Even though Elle was a bit drunk, she still could see us and the surprise that we had made for her. Tears started to roll down her eyes as she saw the dark place that was lighted up by a couple of bulbs and candles. Jean placed the cake on the portable table and it was beautifully lighted up. When Elle started to cry, we suddenly pointed fingers at each other blaming that who had made her cry.

"Congrats Danielle, this is what happens when you get someone drunk" Light pointed out.

"Hello, how else was I supposed, to bring her here. Do you have any other idea's Light instead of this?" Danielle replied.

I was just staring at them as they were arguing on why she was crying. I moved closer to Elle as she was just trying to hide those tears of hers.

"Are you okay Elle, I hope we did not upset you" I asked her while placing one of my hands on her shoulder.

"No, i…it's not t….that" Elle replied as she was still trying to control her tears from flowing. Elle managed to control her tears from flowing as I tried to calm her down. As Elle started to reply, Light and Danielle stopped fighting and started to pay attention towards Elle. "Guys this is so sweet of you guys, I thought everyone forgot the point of the party that I had but I was mistaken. Thanks guys this really means a lot to me" Elle said to us while her eyes were red as though she had run out of tears.

"Sorry if the cake is too small" Jean apologized.

"NO… IT'S PERFECT" Elle replied as she raised her hands to wipe off the last of her tears. We started to sing the HAPPY BIRTHDAY song for her and she seems pretty happy as though all her troubles have just been lifted off her shoulders. That moment wasn't only special to her but it was special to us too even though we were consuming alcohol when we're underage but it was normal. After that we started to have some small talk about how Elle got the idea to throw a party when her parents were away.

CHAPTER 7

DEMANDED PLEASURES

The thing I don't like about life is that time passes by when you are having fun and it slows down when you are suffering. That was the unfairness of life because all good things will eventually come to an end.

It was already 11p.m. ELLE thanked us one last time before heading off inside. Now there's only the four of us left. I was getting really tired. As my eyes started to blink rapidly, the nightmares starts to begin.

I was shocked as I managed to see the girl in white dress hiding behind one of the trees. When I spotted her, she ran away as though she wants me to follow her. I chose to ignore it since I've manage to convince myself that I was a bit drunk, I excused myself as I headed back inside the party. I just needed to wash my face that time to freshen myself up.

As I head inside, people were still dancing and they were full of energy. I am also a teenager but I really don't know where they got the energy from. I spotted Damian as he was chatting with his friends at the side of the stairs. When he saw me looking at him, he instantly turned away his head. He still seem depressed about something, I guess I was too harsh on him. I should listen to Light and start to forgive him. I couldn't spot Elle anywhere in there, I need her to tell me where the restroom is? I start searching for it by myself but there were just too many rooms to look for.

Finally I ended up in front of the door hoping that it was the restroom but when I opened it I was puzzled. I can see Elle in her underwear as she was changing her clothes.

"Hey Maxiel, co…could yo…you help me to get d…dress" Elle asked.

I blushed as I saw her in a black lingerie. There was only one layer that separated her from being completely exposed in front of me. She is still drunk, why isn't she sober. Well if she was sober I would probably get a slap from her so that was the bright side of life right now. I tried avoiding eye contact as I head for the door. When I tried to exit the room she hugged me, in front, behind and spun me around.

"Hey! Maxiel, why are you planning to leave so soon?" Elle asked me while her hands were around my neck.

She suddenly just kissed me. She slides her hands into my back pocket. This is my first time doing this. Her kiss suddenly seemed so desperate as if she needed attention. I know it is wrong but it just felt so good at the moment and I really needed this. Her soft hand was all over me. She unbuttoned my shirt.

"Hahah… look at these abs" Elle pointed out.

I took it off after she unbuttoned my shirt, now her hands were on my chest while the other hand was still in my back pocket. I started to kiss her neck while using one of my hands to support her so that she doesn't fall. Her hands were on my chest.

As everything was going perfect, suddenly my subconscious began to scold me and question myself. Is this right? Do I really want this? This guilt suddenly popped up in my head since it is still wrong for me to take advantage of her.

Am I really going to go through with this? I thought to myself. This is Elle and she is probably drunk. I don't want her to do anything that she might regret so I manage to suck up all the strength and spirit from myself and pushed her onto the bed. When I did that she began to get confused of my action.

"Elle you are quite drunk and I really don't want to be the guy who takes advantages out of drunk girls". I then lifted her up with both of my hands and put her on the bed. My shirt was still on the ground near to the door.

"Now go to bed and don't worry about the party, I don't want you to do anything that you would regret".

All of a sudden, someone opened the door. I started to panic because my body position doesn't seem right. It was Danielle.

As she came into the room, she could see Elle and me. She suddenly dropped the red cup filled with alcohol on the carpet in Elle's bedroom.

"Oh…um… I am sorry, I shouldn't be here right now but I was trying to look for you" she turned shyly.

This isn't her at all. I walk towards her and put one of my hands on her shoulder.

"Are you okay" I asked.

She began to blush and move her eyes away from me trying not to make any eye contact at the moment. She then pushed away my hand and exited the room in a hurry while slamming the door. I was really confused that time. Why would Danielle not look me in the eye or say anything to me at that moment? I leaned down closer to the door and picked up my shirt. When I looked back at Elle, she was already fast asleep. I was just glad that I could resist the temptation. I don't want to hurt her. I put on my shirt first before going back downstairs. I headed to the door and twisted the doorknob clockwise. I walked down the staircase, the moment was really slow for me as I remembered every single detail of the part.

When I reached to the bottom of the staircase, things just got a bit more in inappropriate. There were a lot of people who were just making out like literally everywhere. I guess that's what teenagers like me are supposed to do, guess I am the only outcast around here. The only person that I could see that isn't making out with anyone was Damian. He was just sitting at the other side of the staircase opposite of me. He was avoiding eye-contact. I guess I was just too rough to him. I need to apologize to him but not here, not in public. I will just tell him that his secret is safe with me.

I need to find Danielle, I am really worried about her. As I headed out to the patio, I can see two familiar figures sitting down and having some conversations. It was Light and Jean.

"Hey have you guys seen Danielle around" I asked.

"Nope, sorry bro" Light replied.

Jean just shook her head left to right indicating a no. Why would Danielle run off? As my thoughts were running wild, my vision was starting to blur out. I guess the alcohol was finally kicking in. My balance wasn't also in the correct order. I tried taking out my phone to dial Danielle's number. It was ringing but then she cut the line. It was as though she doesn't want to talk to me at the moment. I started to get worried again, what if she is in trouble? I want to know where she is but my blurred vision and lack of balance is really a huge disadvantage at the moment. With the little stamina and sense that I still have, I tried to think properly where would she be right now if she wasn't at the party. Something tells me that she could be at the place where we celebrated Elle's birthday. I use up all my strength to walk to that place. My eyelids were starting to get heavy as I was walking. True enough she was there, she was sobbing. Why is she sad? I positioned myself behind the tree and was watching her as she pulled out that little pink hanker chief of hers and started wiping off her tears. I managed to gather up enough courage to walk towards her. I tapped her on her shoulder as I approached her and she seemed shocked by that tap as though she had seen a ghost.

"A…are y…you all..right?" I asked her.

I tried my best to keep my tone right but I guess that is one of the alcohols affects. I wish I could speak in proper English right now but my brain just isn't in the right mind. I just had to take a couple of drinks tonight didn't I? RIGHT NOW we were just making eye contact. Our eyes locked at each other and I could see her deep dark blue eyes just filled with sadness and despair. I hated seeing any of my friends go through this kind of emotions. What can I do to help her calm down? I kept on thinking to myself. My eyelids felt so heavy right now and my vision started to go very blur. I felt very sleepy. I leaned towards the bench near the portable table and everything just went black as though my brain just automatically shut down itself.

As everything went black, I appeared in the woods near the school again. No not again, why is this keep on happening to me. I could hear giggles around the dark woods. "Come closer" a soft voice called on upon me. "WHO'S THERE AND WHAT DO YOU WANT FROM ME" I yelled at the top of my lungs. As I looked around me I could see the girl in white dress hiding behind a tree. As I faced her, she ran deep in the woods. The woods were misty that night I managed to see where she was heading thanks to her long blonde hair. Without thinking twice, I ran after her. The cold air hit me as I was chasing her. She was running barefoot. I could catch up with her if I can increase my pace.

As I increased my pace, she starts to sprint. Who is this girl, how could she run that fast. On the way I could see a trail of blood on the ground. Dark clouds began to form in the sky. Thunders and lightning were roaring throughout the sky. I stop as I could not keep my pace up with her. I began to pant really hard as I had used up all of my stamina and energy in order to chase that girl. I was deep in the woods and I really do not know where I am right now. Thunder and lightning began to roar louder in the sky. It was really dark, if only I could see where I am right now. Suddenly, the sky lights up my pathway. There was a big bright crescent moon. I was confused at that time cause at one part of the forest there was lightning and thunder roaring throughout the entire sky but on the other part it seems to be calm and quiet. I choose to follow the bright path but my subconscious and heart ask me to go to the dark side of the forest as though there was something really important that I need to see.

I ignored my feelings and went to the bright side. As I was walking trying to find my way out, I could see the girl in white sitting on a cliff. Huh… I didn't know there was a high cliff around here. As I approached her she suddenly faced towards me. Her legs were crossed. Her pale face looked at me cold heartedly; her bright yellow iris looked dead.

I could see a gold chain hanging around her neck. It spells out DNIM. I am guessing that is her name.

"WHAT DO YOU WANT FROM ME?" I asked her?

Her dead yellow eyes just starred at me "YOU DON'T BELONG HERE, GET OUT NOW". Her tone of voice was soft until she told me to get out, that tone was quite strict.

"Why do you keep following me?" I questioned. She began to turn her body around and faced the ocean. She stood up and looked back at me with a sad face but then she began to smirk. Then she jumped into the ocean. "WAIT…NO… DON'T" I tried to stop.

Suddenly, I could hear someone approaching me. I quickly turn behind me to see who it was. It was a man. A man with messy black hair. His skin was pale as though he was sick. His deep brown iris looks dead. He was wearing a brown coat with a black scarf. I was shocked as he pulled out a gun out of his pocket. I wanted to call out for help but for some reason my voice couldn't work at the moment. I tried but it seems like I was speechless that time. He pointed the gun at me and pulled the trigger. A loud sound was released as he pulled the trigger and everything just went pitch black.

CHAPTER 8

THE HEARTWARMING TRUST

As everything went black, I could hear a voice

"IT IS TIME TO WAKE UP", "WAKE UP", "COME ON WAKE UP".

Those voices filled my head with questions. My eyelids began to open, I could see the sun shining brightly onto my face.

Where am I? I lifted up my left hand to block the sun rays from reaching my face. A familiar shadow was on top of me. It was Light. His face was above my head.

"Come on, are you okay dude?" Light asked.

"Huh… what time is it right now?" I asked grumpily.

The sun rays were just annoying as HELL right now. Why can't today rain? Of all days it just had to be sunny today. Well it is no use complaining right now, because I can't really change the weather now can I?

"It is ten in the morning. Huh… I guess you might have also gotten drunk and decided to crash here too didn't you? Light asked.

I nodded my head in agreement to that statement. I managed to gather up all my stamina to sat up on the bench. What is this soft cotton cloth on my body? My eyes were still trying to adjust to the brightness of the sun.

As everything got clearer, I noticed that the soft cotton cloth was actually a blanket. It must have been Danielle's because she was the only one that I saw last night at this specific spot. Where is she anyway?

"Light have you seen Danielle" I asked.

I am still quite worried about her. Why was she crying yesterday night?

"Yeah Jean is at Danielle's place together with her right now. They are getting ready for tonight's charity ball" Light replied.

Ooooo… I completely forgot about the charity ball. It is okay it is only at night, we still have plenty of time to prepare ourselves. I hope that this hangover wouldn't last that long. I am not drinking anymore that's for sure.

"Umm… Dude we got to be at the tailor's at noon to collect our suites for the ball remember" Light reminded me.

I wished I had time to go home and shower but I currently don't have that choice now. I got up and head inside Elle's house. Surprisingly almost the whole school was still there. Guess I am not the only one who got too drunk last night.

The house was a complete mess; there were red cups and pizza slice almost every corner.

I head up to check up on Elle. I just left her on the bed last night, I hope she's fine.

"Light stay down here for a while, I just need to check on Elle for a second" I ordered Light.

Light nodded. As I head upstairs, I just realized that there were a lot more rooms than I expected it to be. I choose one room that I think that was right and started to twist the doorknob clockwise.

As I opened the door, I could see two teenagers making out. Guess the party isn't over yet. How could they still have that much of stamina and hormones? I guess the house was also messy with all those teenage hormones.

As I entered into the room, a male teen with bushy blonde hair looked at me. His girlfriend was also staring at me in awkwardness. That was the most awkward moment that I have ever felt.

"DUDE, DO YOU MIND" the blonde teen yelled out in irritation.

"Oh… UMM…SORRY" I apologized and looked away from them. Thank HEAVENS there was a blanket on them. As I exited the room, I could hear his girlfriend giggling. Okay now I really got to choose one of these doors carefully, I don't want to get in trouble or look at anything that I wasn't ready for.

I opened another door and there was a teenage girl with shiny brown hair and red highlights in there. She passed out beside the sink and she was covered with her own vomit. Now I finally know what the term SO FAR YET SO CLOSE meant. This is just one huge sleepover.

Come on think properly, which door she could be in? As I was thinking, I suddenly passed by a familiar painting on the wall. It was a painting of a young girl. Yes I finally remembered, the door facing that painting is Elle's room. With excitement, I opened the door and swung it open.

"GAHH….GAAAA" Elle screamed in shock and accidentally fall down beside her bed. She was holding onto a towel.

"Elle are you alright?" I asked.

She started to look to her left and right in confusion. My guess is that she was still in shock. She then looked up at me.

"Dude, you could at least knock before you come in" Elle scolded me.

"Do you want me to help you off the floor?" I asked as I approached her.

"NOOO…STOPP" Elle yelled at me. "I am still naked. When you open the door, I accidentally tripped on my towel" she explained.

I just nodded my head as I looked away.

"Well at least you have no idea what you did yesterday night to me" I told Elle.

"YES… I know". Elle looked down on the ground in shame. She knew what she did and it wasn't appropriate of her. "It's okay, I stopped it before it escalated" I explained.

"WAIT…we didn't slept together?" Elle ask in a soft tone.

"No... I manage to hold myself from doing anything to you because I knew that you were drunk" I explained.

Elle starts to blush. She starts thinking to herself. I just smiled at her innocently and said

"Don't worry, I won't tell anyone about it" I assured her.

She looked at me with happiness. A smile starts to form on her face and without caring about anything else, she got up and hugged me. As she got up, her towel fell on the ground. I was facing towards the door and she hugged me from behind. My heart starts beating hard and I was starting to pant heavily. I try not to look behind.

"Hey Maxiel, thank you" Elle said.

"Elle, could you mind put on a towel" I told her. Thank HEAVENS she couldn't see me blushing right now.

"It is okay, I trust you" Elle said.

That moment when she said that, my heart felt so warm. That feeling of warmth only I could explain. It was so, heartwarming as she said that. No one has ever told me that in person especially when they are not wearing anything.

"I should go now" I excused myself as Elle let go of me. She was still naked behind me. I was so tempted to look behind but I managed to keep it together in me and exited the door without looking behind.

As I exited I could hear Elle giggling behind me. Huh… I guess she was just teasing me all this while but still when she said those words, it kind of open up my heart. As I walked up the staircase, there was a bright smile on my face. Damn it, I couldn't shake off this smile from my face. Why am I smiling like this?

Light noticed my smile and ask me "Is there anything that happened upstairs that I should know about?"

I wonder if I should tell Light anything but I kind of promised that whatever happens between Elle and me should be a secret.

"NO…NOPE" I stammered as I started to blush. Okay I shouldn't have thought about the feeling of when Elle hugged me from behind while she was naked. My heart starts beating hard as I remembered those feelings. My mind was picturing Elle naked but it couldn't create a perfect image since I didn't actually see her.

I stared at Light and it seems that he might have already figured out what had happened. I should really learn how to control my feelings and emotions. I guess I am just so easy to read. Light starts to smirk.

"It's okay Max I won't pressure you on telling" Light said.

Yeah… I am pretty sure the only reason he said that was because he had already figured it out.

There are still a couple of past out teens around us. I don't really feel comfortable talking to Light around here.

"Let's go to the tailor right now, we will be there in time if we leave now" I suggested as he nodded his head in agreement.

As we are about to leave, ELLE was walking down the staircase.

"Do you need any help to clean all of this up?" I asked her.

"No don't worry about it, I had hired some people to help me clean this mess".

"What about your parents, I thought they should be arriving any moment now?" I asked. "That wouldn't be a problem, I got a text from them last night saying that their flight has been postponed till tomorrow afternoon" she replied again.

As she was answering all my questions, my heart rate started to increase. I could remember every single detail of when she hugged me. Why now? I asked myself. I tried to control myself but I couldn't. Why Elle did that? Now I couldn't look at her the same. Elle noticed the redness on my face and she then starts to giggle. She leaned in closer to me and laid her head on the left side of my chest while keeping her left hand on the right side of my chest. Her right hand was in my back pocket again. Now I know why Danielle and she are close friends.

"Leaving so soon Maxiel? She asked while giggling.

I think she can hear my heart rate increasing since her head was directly leaning on my chest.

"YE…YES" I stammered.

I guess at that point Light was just so confused with what was happening.

"Well what ever happened between us earlier and last night is just between us okay" she giggled while looking at Light.

She then let go of me. I dragged Light out of the house as I really couldn't control my heart rate anymore.

As I reached outside, I start to pant heavily.

"You okay dude, what was that?" Light asked.

"I… It was nothing really" I panted.

"Wait did you guys have sex last night?" Light asked.

I nodded my head in denial to that statement. Light began to look at me suspiciously.

"Anyway, let's head to the tailor right now" I told Light while dragging him to the bus stop.

When we arrived at the tailor's, it was already 12.10p.m. The suites that we got seemed expensive and luxurious.

"OKAY… now I am kind of worried about the CHARITY BALL" I stated.

Light nodded in agreement. I am worried because this isn't just some kind of cheap suit, this is like really the good kind of suit. The type that has all this soft and expensive material on it. It means that this charity ball is for the rich and I know when I said it, I don't fit in. When we got the suites, I told Light that we should probably go back to our own respective homes.

"We have to get home and get some rest. Something tells me that tonight is really going to be a long night" I told Light.

"Yeah, let's part here and we will meet up later okay and head over to Danielle's. Jean is staying there for the night" Light informed me.

I nodded as we part way. I was heading home and then suddenly I realized the clouds are beginning to get cloudy. Funny isn't it, wasn't earlier bright and sunny? I guess my wish did come true. I was paying attention to the sky that I didn't realize that I was actually walking towards the highway. As I was walking suddenly a car stopped right in front of me. My reflexes moved my body backwards but it was after the car stopped. It was a black car with stripes on the hood. If he didn't stop, I would have probably got hit.

"HEY, BE CAREFUL NEXT TIME KID, I HAVEN'T GOTTEN MY INSURANCE YET" the man who was driving the car yelled out in anger towards me.

I apologized to the man. I am just glad the suit that I was holding was still alright. Why am I, more worried about the suit then myself. I guess it is because I don't want to disappoint Danielle. How did I end up in the highway wasn't I suppose to walk pass by the park. I guess this is what happens to people when they aren't paying attention to where they are walking. I head back to the right path that I should have been using. I guess I was just enjoying the moment. I really loved the rain for some reason it feels like the rain is a part of me. As I reached home, I put the suit on one side of my room and then I took a cold shower. I haven't taken my shower since this morning. I love showering in cold water, it is like my whole body got awaken from sleep. It is so refreshing. I only liked cold showers I the evening or noon, not in the morning.

After I took my shower, I jumped onto my bed to take a short nap. I know cold water is supposed to be refreshing but something tells me that I am going to need the energy for tonight. I set my alarm an hour and a half ahead. That should be enough for me. I lay my head on the soft pillow and started to wonder about what had happened. I still can remember every detail of when Elle hugged me. It's the words that she uttered into my ear that made my heart felt warm. She said that she TRUSTS me, I really wonder what does that meant. That was the first time someone made my heart feel that way.

As my eyes were about to close suddenly my phone starts vibrating. It was a text from Danielle.

DANIELLE: Guys the BALL starts at 8p.m. so be here by 7p.m.

LIGHT: Okay, Maxiel and I just got our suites from the tailor earlier.

DANIELLE: THAT'S GREAT!!!

JEAN: You guys should probably have a short nap since yesterday took out all of our energy.

MAXIEL: Tell me about it.

As I replied to the group, I just went and closed my eyes hoping that tonight would be a success like yesterday. I should probably stop thinking about yesterday and focus on today if only Elle didn't hug earlier, I would not have any problems sleeping. After what had happened last night, it is best to just forget about it. My mind was still revolving around all of yesterday's incidents but I manage to control myself and force myself to go to bed. I only have an hour and a half to sleep, might as well use it to the fullest. My eyes shut as everything else went pitch black.

CHAPTER 9

THE CHARITY BALL

BEEP! BEEP! BEEP, my alarm starts ringing. I was so sleepy that my eyes couldn't even open. I finally managed to open my eyes and looked outside the window. The sky was still cloudy. If it is going to rain, it's best to be asleep.

NO... I can't the charity ball is tonight and I promised Danielle that I would be there. I grabbed my phone that was beside me to check the time.

WAIT...WHAT, I slept for more than an hour and a half. It is already 5.30p.m.

My phone was filled with messages and three miscalls. The first message was at 4.35p.m., it was from Jean.

JEAN: Guys please tell me you are awake by now?

LIGHT: YEAH! WHAT'S UP?

JEAN: There is a slight problem with the CHARITY BALL.

LIGHT: What happened?

DANIELLE: We need extra waiters. We miscalculated the number of people that would be attending. It was more than we anticipated.

LIGHT: What's your point?

DANIELLE: Could you and Maxiel be waiters for an hour please? IT'S AN EMERGENCY!!!

LIGHT: SURE …why not? BUT YOU OWE US DANIELLE!!!

DANIELLE: YEAH SURE!!! Where's Maxiel?

JEAN: Yeah we also need him.

LIGHT: He is probably still sleeping. Never mind just tell us what we have to do then I will inform him later.

DANIELLE: Be here by 6.30p.m. I will brief you guys on some things.

LIGHT: OKAY GOT IT!!!

The messages then ended at 5p.m. I got three miscalls from Light after that. Okay, we must be there at 6.30p.m., I can make it. I quickly jumped out of bed and took a quick shower.

After my shower I called Light but he wasn't picking up. I tried again and again but he was still not picking up. Finally as I put on my suit, I got a call from him. I reached out to my phone and picked it up.

LIGHT: Sorry about earlier, my phone was on silent mode.

MAXIEL: Where are you right now?

LIGHT: Still at home.

MAXIEL: OKAY LET'S MEET AT THE BUS STOP AT 6.10P.M. OKAY?

LIGHT: No problem. By the way we are going to be waiters for an hour so let's meet Danielle once we reach there.

MAXIEL: YEAH I know, got it.

I hung up the phone and did some final preparations. The suit fit me perfectly.

I headed downstairs and surprisingly my mum was there. She does not normally come home this early so this was a surprise.

"HEY THERE, WHERE ARE YOU GOING?" she asked excitedly as she has not seen me in a suit.

"I am going to a charity ball at DANIELLE'S place for the night" I answered.

She nodded her head.

"Well have fun then. Ohh… and don't forget to take an umbrella, it looks like it is about to rain" my mom ordered.

I nodded my head. Something is missing what had I forgotten. I headed back upstairs and grabbed a watch. A suit is incomplete without a watch. There it all seems perfect now I thought to myself.

I walked downstairs and yelled out "BYE MOM!!" and then she replied "GOODBYE AND CAREFUL ON YOUR WAY TO DANIELLE'S HOUSE".

I twisted the doorknob clockwise and exited the house. I got to meet Light at the bus stop at 6.10p.m. Now is already 6, if I run, I could make it. I ran with all my might, it is really hard to run in a suit. As I reached the bus stop, I could see Light in his suit too. He was waving at me. I started to pant really hard.

"Max, you alright" Light asked.

"Yeah, I just need to catch my breath for a second" I answered him.

It took a while but I finally managed to catch my breath. My heart rate was slowly decreasing as I manage to calm myself down. As the bus arrived, we got on without any hesitation. Sure it seems weird to be wearing a suit while riding on a bus but who cares.

As we arrived at our destination, we walked slowly to Danielle's house. Her house is definitely more impressive then Elle's house. It is like five times bigger than Elle's house. We rang the doorbell and then there was a voice coming out of a speaker. "PLEASE FACE THE CAMERA". We did so and then the gate opened. The distance between the front gate and the main door was about the length of two school buses.

As we stood in front of the main door, I twisted the doorknob clockwise and entered into the house together with Light.

As we entered we were greeted by a man with black hair and deep blue eyes. He was in his late forties but he seems young and fit for his age. He was wearing black suit that goes along with his watch. It was Mr. Fond. He is Danielle's dad.

"AH… hello there you must be Danielle's friends", Mr. Fond stared at us. We nodded.

"If you are looking for Danielle, she is currently with her friend in her room" Mr. Fond stated.

"Can we see her?" Light asked.

"Sure, just head upstairs and go left. You will then see a door with Danielle's name on it" Mr. Fond replied while pointing to the huge staircase.

"Thanks Mr. Fond" I said.

He then nodded at us with a smile. We headed upstairs. Now I know why he gave us direction to Danielle's room, when we reached upstairs there were just so many rooms. I started to scratch my head in confusion.

Light grabbed my shoulder "Don't get stressed for all this little things, you need to relax".

"I am relaxed, what makes you think that I am stressed?" I asked.

"Well if I am not mistaken, whenever you think too much, you will scratch the back of your head" Light answered.

I looked at him in a sarcastic way and lifted up my eyebrow. We used the directions that Mr. Fond gave us and we looked for Danielle's room. It took us about five minutes to search for it. Finally, we arrived at the room that has Danielle's name on it. I was excited for some reason. I twisted the doorknob clockwise and swung it open. "SCREAM".

As I opened the door I could hear a couple of girls screaming. It was Danielle and Jean as they were changing. They were using Danielle's bed sheets as cover. Light and I were just staring. Even though they were using those bed sheets as cover, we could still see a bit of exposure.

"CAN'T YOU GUYS KNOCK NEXT TIME" Danielle yelled out.

Yeah I guess I should start learning how to knock people's door before I actually swing them open. Why whenever I open a door, there must be some naked or half naked people in there? But seriously what are the odds of me opening the door when someone is changing their clothes twice in a day. This got me remembering of Elle and what she did to me this morning.

"ARE YOU GUYS JUST GOING TO STAND THERE?" Jean yelled out.

"NO...We won't" Light answered.

Light then entered into the room approaching them. I was in a state of confusion as he got closer to them.

"NOO... THAT IS NOT WHAT WE MEANT. GET OUT!!!" Danielle screamed in embarrassment.

Light just look at them and smirk. They were trying their best to hold on onto those sheets so that their underwear won't be exposed in front of us. As Light approached them, I grabbed his hand I pulled him out of the room.

As we exited the room, I could hear someone running towards the door and locking it. They should have locked it earlier so that we know that we weren't supposed to enter.

"GUYS WAIT FOR US AT THE KITCHEN" Danielle yelled.

All of the sudden I could hear them laughing, I have a bad feeling about this. They are up to something. Either that or they just find it funny that we entered while they were changing their clothes. Please let it be the second one.

Light and I head towards the kitchen. It was empty for the moment. After a few minutes of fooling around, JEAN and DANIELLE walked in. They were stunning. Jean was wearing a bright blue dress with a black ribbon on it while Danielle was wearing a slim fit dress that follows her body shape and it has a slit cutting on it. The way they looked at us was absolutely weird it is like they were up to something.

"Guys follow me" Danielle ordered us.

We followed her into a room on the second floor. As she opens the door, there were two waiters outfit hanging on the door. Okay I kind off know where this is going.

"Guys change into this uniform now" Danielle ordered.

Jean was just giggling at the corner.

"Aren't you guys going to leave the room" Light asked.

"Well you guys saw us in our underwear, it is time for us to return the favor, don't you think?" Danielle replied while locking the door so that no one could enter the room. "What make you think that we will change here?" I asked.

Danielle just looked at me with a smirk. She then leaned in closer to me and whispered "Didn't someone had some fun with Damian yesterday night" Danielle smirked.

At that moment, I was shocked. She knew what happened.

"Well played Danielle" I replied.

Jean approached Light and then whispered something into his ear. His eyes began to open widely in utter shock. Guess the two of them have dirt on us huh.

"Now do you guys want to change in front of us?" Danielle asked. We just nodded our head and sighed.

There was nothing that we could do since they have cornered us. HUH...Girls, their memories are so strong and detailed. Danielle and Jean then took chairs and sit in front of us. I then began to take off my clothes first. I strip till I was only wearing my red boxers with black headlines on it. I then raised both my hands halfway and said "Are you guys happy now?" I could clearly see that Danielle was trying to avoid eye contact with me. She was starting to blush. I could use this to my advantage. I began to play with Danielle's emotions.

I approached Danielle and held the chair handle. "What's wrong isn't this what you wanted?" I asked. She was looking away from me that time.

"YO...YOU A..RE TOO C..CLOSE" Danielle stammered.

I began smirking at her. At that moment I could see her face began to turn red.

Suddenly, someone swung the door wide open and I could hear a loud voice yelling.

"HEY GIRLS READY FOR THE BALL". It was Elle. This day is just starting to get more ridiculous. Of all times why now? Elle look at Light and me.

"Danielle I didn't know you were having this kind of party" Elle turned in confusion. I turn around and look at Light as he was also in his grey boxers. He was trying to put on the waiters shirt.

"Ohh… Light those white shirt and grey boxers suits you well" Elle stated.

Light ignored Elle and continued putting on his clothes. My mind was kind of lost for the moment I thought Danielle had locked the door.

"Didn't you lock the door?" Jean asked Danielle. Danielle was also confused at the moment because she thought she had locked the door. She then pushed me away for a moment. Her hand was cold and it felt so comfy. She approached the door to check on the lock.

"The lock is broken" Danielle stated.

Seriously of all rooms why must we be in the room where the lock is busted? I thought to myself.

I was just standing there in my boxers giving everyone the view of me when I am half naked. As my thoughts suddenly came back to me, I quickly took the waiters uniform and changed.

"Take your time, don't rush. We have all already seen you in your red boxers" Elle stated.

Ughh…screw it, she is right anyway. After I put on the waiters uniform, Danielle gave us some briefing. She told us that we need to only serve the early birds for a while since her dad had to do some last minute call. Her dad had hired some waiters last minute and they will only arrive at 7.50p.m. Which is ten minutes before the CHARITY BALL begins.

As we head downstairs, Mr. Fond approached us and thanked us for our assistance. We told him that it wasn't a big deal and he nodded at us with appreciation.

We were asked to serve some refreshments at first. Danielle taught us the posture that we should make while we were serving. Our left hand must be tied to our back while our right hand must hold the tray of refreshments.

The crowd started coming in at 7p.m. and we started serving them. Their clothes look so ridiculously expensive no wonder Danielle had us wearing suites. If it weren't for her I would have just probably wore a shirt and a pair of skinny jeans which could be the cause of me getting kicked out of the party.

Time passes by as we served. At 7.45p.m., Danielle and Jean called us to get changed again since the waiters that her dad hired had arrived a bit early.

Now we can enjoy the BALL.

CHAPTER 10
HEARTFELT RYTHM

We entered into the same room only this time, we had some privacy. Danielle and Jean were waiting outside as Light and I were changing back to our suits. We knew that the door lock was busted but we don't care since they have already seen us in our boxers.

After putting on our suits, we opened the door. Danielle and Jean were wearing some kind of mask. I was puzzled at that time.

"Yeah I forgot to tell you guys but we are all required to wear a mask" Danielle stated.

Danielle was wearing a silver mask with golden patterns on it while Jean was wearing a gold mask with silver patterns. It really suits them. Jean then handed us our own masks. Light has a black mask with golden patter while mine was matching Danielle's one.

"You are going to be my date for the night that is why I got us a matching set" Danielle stated.

After putting on the mask that was given to us, we headed downstairs. Everyone present there was wearing masks as well.

After a couple of minutes, I could hear a noise. It is like someone was hitting a glass with a spoon. It was Mr. Fond, he was going to give a toast.

"Everyone thank you for coming to support this charity. As you all know the donations are going to be used to create an animal sanctuary. You all are doing a wonderful job trying to help and protect the wildlife. It is our job to do so in order for the survival of animal species. This is so that our future generations may be able to understand the beauty of nature created by GOD. Once again I would like to thank you all for your donations and please also have a good time here. I hope you all would enjoy the stay" Mr. Fond stated while raising his glass in front of everyone.

CLAP *CLAP* *CLAP* everyone started to clap. Then the classic music started to play. Danielle grabbed my hand and pulled me to the dance floor. Jean did the same to Light. We were dancing to the beat as my hands were on Danielle's hip and her hands were around my neck.

As we were dancing I asked Danielle something "Danielle why were you crying last night" I asked.

Danielle's eyes suddenly began to widen. I could see it even though she was wearing a mask. It looks as if she doesn't want to talk about it.

"It's okay if you don't want to talk about it but know this I am always here for you if you need me and so is Jean and Light because that is what friends are for" I stated.

Danielle just smiled as I spun her around. As I spun her around I noticed two odd people on the dance floor. The girl in particular, she was wearing a very familiar white dress. She was also wearing a golden mask with black patterns on it.

It then shocked me as I saw the same golden necklace hanging from her neck. DNIM, it was the girl who kept on haunting me.

What does DNIM means? Who is she? But I only managed to see her in a flash. As someone blocked my view and passes me it turned out to be a completely different girl. I turned my head trying to search for her but I couldn't. Danielle noticed my odd behavior.

"Maxiel are you alright?" she asked.

"Yeah, I am. Do you mind excusing me for a while" I excused myself and searched the dance floor for the girl.

As I was passing by people, I tried to focus on them to spot the girl but she wasn't there.

What happened to her? Who is she? I thought to myself.

As my head was clouded with these thoughts, someone tapped me on the shoulder. I was caught off guard and it shocked me for a moment. It was Light. "Max are you okay?" Light asked.

"YEAH, I AM" I replied.

"What were you searching for earlier?" He questioned again.

"NO...NEVERMIND. I thought I just saw something" I answered.

Light looked at me and he knew that I was overthinking stuff again.

"Come on join us" Light invited.

I nodded to him. He then brought me to a table where Jean and Danielle were chatting. They removed their masks and they seemed to be having the time of their life. I sat beside Danielle while Light sat beside Jean. I was facing Light and Danielle was facing Jean.

"Everything okay, Maxiel?" Jean asked.

I nodded at her.

"HMM… that was the first time someone left me alone on the dance floor" Danielle stated.

I look at her and start smiling.

"I am really sorry that I left you on the dance floor. You were so beautiful out there that I could not control myself and that is why I left you so I could wash off the droll on my face" I stated.

Everyone was just looking at me with a puzzled face. Danielle's jaw dropped as she didn't expect that out of me. She was silent for about a few seconds. The atmosphere began to get a bit awkward.

Why did I say that? Suddenly, someone came and pulled up a chair next to me. It was Elle.

As Elle sat down beside me, she broke the silence and awkwardness between all of us. She started asking is everything okay between all of us.

"Are you guys okay? You guys seem a bit shocked" Elle said.

We all just nodded our heads with a smile. Elle then leaned closer to me and whispered,

"Hey Maxiel, what happened between us is still a secret isn't it?" she asked.

"Nothing happened between us" I whispered back to her.

She starts to smirk. I looked at Light and Jean, they weren't paying any attention to us because they were having their own chat. I turned over to Danielle and she seems to be busy with her phone. Thank HEAVENS no one heard what we were whispering. I really don't want to get questioned a lot. Elle was just staring at me and this makes me feel so uncomfortable. Suddenly from below the table, I could feel someone touching me. It was Elle. I stared at her in irritation but she just kept on going. Finally, I pushed her hand away from my knee.

"Elle please don't do this, especially here" I whispered to her.

Her eyes began to dim as if she is now sad and depressed right now. The thoughts of her bare body touching my back began to cloud up my mind but I chose to ignore those feelings. What are these feelings, it is like I crave for love but I don't go around asking for it.

"OHHH…um excuse me for a moment, I have to use the restroom" Elle excused herself as she walked away from our table.

Suddenly Danielle quickly stood up.

"Guys let's go somewhere else quick" she ordered.

Light and Jean were completely shocked as they were so deep into their conversation. Everyone rushed out following Danielle. Where is she bringing us this time? Why all of the sudden? I thought to myself.

As we got outside we were all shocked by the weather. It was raining heavily. Thunder and lightning were roaring throughout the sky. Ughhh… I forgot to bring the umbrella my mom asked me to bring. Why didn't I bring it?

"HOW COULD YOU SLEEP WITH ELLE LAST NIGHT" Danielle yelled out.

This is shocking for me because why would she ask that type of question in a time like this? Light and Jean were just staring at us with their eyes wide open.

"BOTH OF US WERE DRUNK BUT NOTHING HAPPENED. WE DIDN'T HAVE SEX" I replied.

Our voices weren't that clear since the raindrops were too loud but we could still hear each other as we focused.

"STOP LYING MAXIEL, I SAW YOU MAKING OUT WITH HER YESTERDAY NIGHT" Danielle insisted.

At that moment, I just stood still because it has all come back to me now. Is Danielle jealous? I realized this as I could see her eyes starting to tear but she is controlling her emotions at the moment.

"We just made out, than I pushed her away since I knew she was drunk and I don't want to make her feel bad about herself. If I had sex with her, I wouldn't have been sleeping on the bench this morning" I replied.

Light and Jean knew that the atmosphere around us is getting more tense. Suddenly, Jean grabbed my hand and Light grabbed Danielle's hand. They pulled all of us to the rain. It was cold.

"WHY THE HELL DID YOU GUYS DID THAT?" Danielle questioned.

"You really need to enjoy life a bit you know" Light replied.

You know I think Light is right, all this while I have been so deep in thought that I haven't really been able to enjoy the little things. Danielle looked irritated as she was soaking in the rain. I approached her and hugged her.

"You know that I have always liked you right but, I just don't have the courage to tell you until now".

Danielle looked at me in shock. Light then took some water and splashed on me. I let go of Danielle at that moment.

"Okay I am so going to get you for that" I said to Light with a smirk on my face.

"COME ON DANIELLE JOIN US. DON'T TELL ME A PRINCESS LIKE YOU COULD NOT HAVE FUN HUH!!!" Jean provoked Danielle.

All of a sudden I could see a smile form on Danielle's face. It was like a huge burden had been lifted up from her shoulders. I tackled Light and then dropped onto the ground. Jean tried to kick Danielle but she ended falling "GAHAH".

Her scream was funny but adorable in some ways. Light helped her to get up. We were all having a good time that moment. Jean and Danielle were pushing us on the ground. Thank Heavens the ground is filled with soft carpet grass and not cement. It was fun, it was the best moment of my life. It turns that we all could have fun whenever we want and the only thing that we need is the right people at the right time and in the right place.

Even though the weather wasn't suitable to play outside but we still had fun. It was like being a child all over again. After being soaking wet outside, we decided to head back in so that we would not catch a cold.

We used the backdoor to enter into Danielle's house. The backdoor is connected to the kitchen which leads to a hall that has a hidden staircase to the top floor. We used that way to sneak upstairs. Danielle pointed us to two restrooms. She told us to take a quick hot bath. She even gave us towels for it. We let Light and Jean to go on first to take the bath. I brought Danielle to the hall for a while. Damn, it is cold especially when you are wet and the whole house is air conditioned.

"It's okay Maxiel you don't have to explain anything. I was just quite emotional just now. I mean it is your wish to sleep with anybody that you want to and I don't have the right to stop you from doing anything" Danielle stated before I could say anything.

Her tone of voice was soft and she started smiling at me.

"Well look who is acting tough right now" I joked around.

This isn't the right moment to tell anything to her since it was freezing cold and I was chattering like crazy. I just nodded at her and headed back into the room. Danielle did the same as we then locked the doors. After a couple of minutes watching TELEVISION, Light came out of the shower all dressed up. He was wearing a blue T-SHIRT that goes along with a pair of sweatpants. "Your turn, Oh, and I brought you spare clothes too" light said.

"When did you bring spare clothes?" I asked.

"Remember the bag that I always carry around me, yeah inside the bag I always bring three spare clothes with me just in case. You could borrow mine if you want" Light stated.

I nodded while thanking him. As I entered into the shower, I strip everything off. The feeling of the warm water hitting my skin is just so comfortable. I mean who wouldn't agree after being wet in the cold rain. I just enjoyed that hot shower. After the shower, I headed out with my towel. I wondered how did Light changed in there as it was crammed up.

As I came out with my towel, I could see Light, Jean and Danielle on the bed watching television. I just went to the corner of the room and changed my clothes. Light handed me a white shirt and some blue shorts.

"Hey I brought some movies, which one do you guys want to watch?" Danielle asked while holding three DVDs in her hand.

All the movies were in different genres. It was either romance, horror and fictional. We all agreed on watching the horror movie because there isn't any better feeling than watching a horror movie under the blankets in this weather.

The television in that room was quite big. After I put in the DVD into the VCR, I jumped on the bed with the three of them. The bed was a king size bed so it fit all of us. The blanket was so soft and comfortable. Nothing could beat the moment. Danielle was sitting beside me while Light was in between Danielle and Jean. After a couple of minutes throughout the movie someone knocked on the door. It was Mr. Fond.

"Yes Daddy, do you need anything?" Danielle asked.

Mr. Fond just smiled at us as he saw us watching a movie.

"Nothing DEAR, I was just wandering what were all of you doing. The charity BALL had just finished and if you guys want supper, you all are most welcome to the kitchen and help yourselves" Mr. Fond stated.

"Thanks Daddy, we all will so you don't have to worry about us" Danielle replied to her dad with a big wide smile.

"OHH…I almost forgot, it seems like it is quite a downpour outside so I highly recommend that you guys stay here for the night. I have already called and informed your parents so don't worry about it" Mr. Fond stated.

Danielle got up off the bed and ran to her dad to give him a big hug. Her dad just smiled at us and hugged his only daughter back. Mr. Fond let go of Danielle as he then closed the door. Danielle then jumped onto the bed and joined us. The moment was just so comfortable that I wish it could last forever.

Unfortunately, not all good things last forever. Halfway throughout the movie, another knock came onto the door but this time that person didn't wait for any reply or welcome. The door just swung wide open. It looked like someone familiar. As the light entered into the dark room, my vision started to blur. My eyes tried to adjust to the brightness that had just been flashed onto my eyes. Then the shadow standing in front of us turns out to be very familiar.

It took a while and then we found out that it was Elle. What is she doing here? How did she find us in this room among all the rooms?

"GUYS WHY DIDN'T YOU INVITE ME HERE?" Elle asked in frustration.

I know we love Elle and all as a friend but we need space sometimes too. I mean the four of us are normally a group and are always together. It just doesn't seem right Elle had suddenly joined the group.

In this case, Elle is like the fifth wheel as she always interrupted us while we were hanging out. But, then she is our friend and we have to be fair to her to in a way. We just put aside our feelings for the moment and invited her to join us cause in a way the more the merrier right?

At that moment my phone starts vibrating. It was a text from my mom.

MOM: Honey, are you staying at Danielle's for the night?

MAXIEL: Yup, Mr. Fond insisted that all of us stayed for the night because it's raining heavily outside.

MOM: I told you to take an umbrella, didn't I?

MAXIEL: I doubt that umbrella was going to help anyway.

MOM: Okay never mind just take care okay.

MAXIEL: Okay, goodnight mom

MOM: Goodnight!!!

I then placed my phone on the table beside me.

"Who was that" Jean asked.

"It was my mom" I replied.

She then just nodded and went back watching the movie.

Elle was just in the middle between all of us but it was quite comfy since the whole house is air conditioned and the blankets just kept us warm. The rain outside isn't really getting any better.

How did this happen? Wasn't today morning was just hot as hell? After the movie, all of us went down for a midnight snack. The kitchen was as huge as always. There were stocks of food in Danielle's refrigerator.

We choose to take out some frozen food and heat it up in the oven. We heated up five frozen pizzas. Each one of us had our own flavor but we shared anyway. It was already about one in the morning. We decided to head up to bed. Danielle gave Light and me the guest room to sleep in while Jean and Elle would sleep in her room.

Light and I headed to the guest room. Even the guest room is huge and it has its own FLAT SCREEN TV.

I was quite tired so I head on to bed while Light decided to use the FLAT SCREEN TV. As I lay down on my bed, the girl in the white dress popped up in my head. WHO IS SHE? WHAT DOES SHE WANT FROM ME? I could still remember the gold necklace hanging around her neck that time. Her name must be DNIM. I tried to forget everything but it just doesn't seem to work. I felt tired but my head isn't going to let me sleep. "Dude, are you okay?" Light asked.

I just stared at him and nodded.

"You should really stop overthinking stuff. By the way are you ready for the big football match on Tuesday?" Light questioned.

"Wait what, what match?" I asked.

"How could you forget about the big game. Our school is competing against the south side" Light stated.

How could I forget about such an important thing? My head began to get clouded with thoughts again. Light noticed that I am overthinking.

"If you need to talk, I am here for you cause that's what bro's are for" Light stated.

"It's okay, I am just having a bit trouble going to bed" I replied.

"If you want, I could go for another movie or you could just count sheep" Light stated.

I just looked at him with a smile. I closed my eyes and started counting sheep. I wonder how it works. No I must concentrate I must count sheep in order to go to bed. Why must it be sheep? Seriously, this is what happens when I want to go to bed. My thoughts will be so active at that moment while during the day it is most likely to be asleep. I try to focus on the sheep that are jumping on the fence. One sheep, two sheep, three sheep. It still didn't work I guess I need a glass of water. I could see that Light is already fast asleep and I was jealous of it. I got up from bed and walked down the staircase.

I then head to the kitchen to grab a glass of water, hopefully now I could go to bed peacefully.

As I was about to walk back up, I could hear some people talking. I followed those sounds and ended up in front of a room. The door was slightly open. I could hear two voices from the room. I took a peek and I could see Mr. Fond talking to somebody. I could not see the other person since the door is blocking the view.

"Why are you doing this?" the guy asked.

"We have no choice, our company is currently facing some downfall" Mr. Fond replied.

"I need the money. I have a daughter who is in the hospital right now. She is barely surviving" the man stated in a frustrated tone of voice.

"I am sorry Bill but I have to let you go" Mr. Fond replied.

All of a sudden I could see the other guy's hand. He took a vase that was beside Mr. Fond and smashed it to pieces. After I saw that I immediately ran back upstairs. I could hear Mr. Fond shouting "OUT, GET OUT NOW". What was that all about? I ignored it since it has nothing to do with me. I jumped onto the bed and believe it or not my eyes suddenly felt heavy and everything around me just went blank.

I then awoke in the same dark woods again. OH…NO NOT THIS AGAIN. This time it was a bit different. The girl in the white dress was just sitting on the same cliff again but what was beside her that shocked me. She was holding a gun in her hand and she pointed to the dark figure or stuff beside her with the gun. I approached the dark figure that was beside her.

I tried to adjust my eyes to the darkness around me and it took some time but I finally did it. IT WAS A CORPSE. IT WASN'T JUST ANY CORPSE IT WAS ME. At that moment I took a step back and I tripped on a branch that was behind me. The girl then look at me with her innocent eyes. She then smirked while pointing the gun towards me. I tried to run but my legs were heavy at that moment. Off all times why now? Why can't I move this time? Why is this keep on happening to me? My head was running through with all this negative thoughts at that moment.

The girl then pulled the hammer of the gun down aiming for my head. As she pulled the trigger a loud BANG sound appeared. As the bullet hit me everything just went black. As black as night.

CHAPTER 11

UNEEDED SUPPORT

Again I woke up as the sun rays hit my face. Light had opened the window and he was just watching the television. What time did he wake up?

"So did you have a good sleep?" Light asked.

I was just trying to wake myself up but I couldn't. My body really needed the rest. Do I really have to get up now?

It is really comfortable as the whole room is air conditioned. For some reason I knew that I should not oversleep. I took a peek at the time and it was already ten in the morning. I am so glad that today is a Sunday. I managed to gather all my energy and forced myself to wake up. Danielle gave us some disposable toothbrush.

As I went to the washroom, I took one out of its packet and put toothpaste on it.

After I brushed my teeth Light told me that we are invited to have breakfast downstairs. I told Light to go ahead first because I need to clean up the room a bit.

As I was making the bed I could hear someone crying in the other room. I was curious. That voice sounded so familiar. I headed to the particular room. As I was outside, I twisted the doorknob clockwise and took a peek to see who it was. After peeking, I immediately knew who she was. She was facing the window and it seems like she is trying to control herself from crying. It was Jean. She was sitting at the corner of the bed I approached her and she noticed me.

"Please just go away for a while Maxiel" she ordered.

I ignored her and just sat beside her.

"Do you want to talk?" I asked.

"No, I just need time alone" Jean cried.

Her eyes seemed like she really needed help. I want to help her. I want to know why she's crying so that I could help her.

"You have to tell me what is going on so that I could help you" I told her.

She just ignored me.

"Jean you really have to tell me what is going on" I said to her.

"I know that you meant well and all but this is my problem and it's personal. Please just leave me alone" Jean stated.

I look at her and then remembered something. Remember the time when i said that people with bright smile often faces depression. They sometimes tend to cry alone and keep their feelings to themselves. Sometimes behind those smiles lies a deep lie that they constantly tell themselves. Hmm... who would have known that Jean is one of those people. I hug her in attempt to calm her down. She was completely shocked by what I did.

"Remember we are always going to care for you even if you push us away" I said.

Jean just looked at me as she managed to calm herself down.

"I hope this doesn't affect your opinion of me" she said.

"Light, Danielle and I are always here for you so you don't have to hide your feelings from us. All of us are actually as messed up as you that's why we need each other" I replied to her.

Jean looked at me in appreciation as she returned the hug back to me.

"Thanks Maxiel, I think I really needed that" Jean said.

"Now come let's head down for breakfast, they are waiting for us" I suggested.

Jean just nodded in agreement as she took a couple of tissues to wipe off her tears. As Jean and I got to the bottom of the staircase, we could see that Light and Danielle are on the sofa playing with their smartphones.

"Are you guys ready for breakfast" Danielle said out in excitement as she dragged all of us to the kitchen. On the table there were five plates and on top of them all there were pancakes.

Not the normal type of pancakes, for some reason this seem quite fancy. As we all sat down on the table Light asked Danielle and Jean about Elle.

"By the way where is Elle?" Light asked looking at them.

"She is still sleeping, she is just tired" Jean replied.

In front of our pancakes, there was maple syrup. Each one of us had our own maple syrup. I think we should open one and just share. No one is going to take one whole bottle of maple syrup well unless they want DIABETES. During breakfast Danielle told us about how their night was.

For some reason as soon as Danielle mentioned that I remembered something. The dream that I had, what does it mean? Why I kept on having this type of dream? It is like I am given some kind of warning or message. Whatever it is, I am just going to keep myself away from the woods beside the school. Those woods still haunt me even though I am not near it. Well on second thought, should I investigate those woods. Maybe I could get some kind of clue from there. No, I have seen a lot of horror movies to know what would happen to someone if they go inside the woods all by themselves. My only choice right now is to ignore those weird places.

"Hey are you alright? You seem quiet" Light asked me.

All the three of them were just staring at me and was waiting for an answer.

"Yeah I am alright, just not enough sleep I think" I answered.

I don't want to tell them anything at the moment. I don't want them to worry about me. I just have to figure this out for myself. After breakfast, Jean, Light and I head home as we waved goodbye to Danielle. We also thanked Mr. Fond for the hospitality as he got downstairs. The three of us separated as we got to an intersection. The sky today seemed so calm. It was sunny.

As I got home, I straight away went and took a shower. I showered with cold water so that all the cells on my body could wake up and be fresh. After I got out of the shower my phone starts to vibrate. It was a text message from Jean.

JEAN: Guys Light and I saw some posters about a carnival that is held on Tuesday. Do you guys want to go?

DANIELLE: Yeah sure I am not busy. At night right?

JEAN: YEAH… it is at night so we have a lot of time to get ready after school.

I then thought to myself and then remembered about the football game that I was going to compete this Tuesday. I then replied to them about the game.

MAXIEL: I can't. I have a football match on that day.

LIGHT: Your match starts at 6p.m, so if you want we could go around 9p.m to the carnival. That is my suggestion but only if you agree to it.

DANIELLE: Come on Maxiel, don't leave us hanging.

I thought to myself for a while. Will I be tired by then? Should I go? It took me a while but then I had made my choice. I want to spend as much time as I can with my friends so I accepted Light's suggestion. I then replied them back.

MAXIEL: Sure but after the game.

JEAN: Okay so Light and I will get the tickets first okay.

DANIELLE: THANKS LIGHT AND JEAN!!!

MAXIEL: Yeah thanks.

LIGHT: No Problem

After that I placed my phone beside the desk. Ughh.. Why tomorrow is a school day? This weekend was fun that I couldn't get enough of it.

I can't wait for Tuesday; something tells me that Tuesday is going to be fun.

I slept in the afternoon and then woke up around 5p.m. I was happy since I had no more nightmares, well at least for now.

At night, I had dinner with my mom. She bought fast food again. We had small talks about the CHARITY BALL. I will tell her that but

I won't tell her about the party. That is the last thing any mom should know.

After dinner, I headed upstairs. This is normally the time where I complete some last minute assignments. Yes I have a habit of doing homework at the last second. It took me two hours to complete it but as soon as I was done, it made me really happy cause I don't have to stress about getting detention from any of the teachers. Tomorrow is Monday and Monday is really a long day. I hate Mondays. I looked at my schedule. HMM…nothing interesting. I checked the time it was already a quarter past one.

Damn…I am so going to have trouble waking up tomorrow. I jumped onto my bed and lay my head onto the soft pillow. Looking back, I was glad that I was able to help Jean a bit. I am a bit worried about Jean I just hope that she doesn't hide her feelings from us. Then all of a sudden Danielle popped into my mind. I was never able to tell her how I feel yet, maybe I should tell her at the carnival on Tuesday after the game.

All those memories of us playing in the rain and how we watched a horror movie under the blanket really made my heart warm. It was like the best moment that I ever had so far and I know that there are more yet to come when I am with them. My eyes felt heavy as I turn facing to my window. All of a sudden, words started appearing on the window again. It spelled out YOU DON'T BELONG HERE!!! GET

OUT NOW!!! It was written in blood and this really freaked me out as I got up panting really hard. My heart rate increased rapidly and I started to pant really hard.

I look at the window again and there was nothing. Am I really losing my mind? It is okay it will be gone. I pulled down the binds to cover the window.

I tried to calm myself down by remembering some funny stuff. Believe it or not it worked. My eyes just close and everything then went black. It felt peaceful here.

CHAPTER 12

SILENT HORROR

BEEP, BEEP, BEEP, as the annoying sound of my alarm starts beeping I knew that it was time to wake up.

I checked the time and it was six already in the morning. Well guess it is time to wake up and prepare to go to school. I opened the binds to see the outside view. The day is getting brighter, I hope today goes well. I head to the restroom to brush my teeth and to take a shower.

I took out a green shirt and a pair of black skinny jeans. I head downstairs for breakfast.

My mom was sitting at the table with some omelets on a plate.

As I came down she starts to smile.

"That's weird, Light isn't with you. Did you get up yourself today?" my mom asked.

I just sat down on the table and nodded my head. Speaking of Light, where is he? This is weird. He would normally sneak into my room. I guess there is a first for everything.

"I guess he must have woken up late" I replied.

"That doesn't sound like him" my mom said.

I just nodded and took an omelet and placed it on top of my plate.

After breakfast, I head off to wait outside as the bus will be arriving in three more minutes.

"OH… Honey do not forget to take your umbrella this time" my mom yelled.

"Thanks mom" I replied. Luckily she reminded me. I will not repeat the same mistake again. I know it's fun to get soaking wet in the rain with your friends and all but it is seriously cold as ice. I'm a bit surprised that none of us caught a cold, it must be thanks to our high immune system.

As I waited outside, I looked up at the sky and it was cloudy and nice. It must be rainy season this time.

After a couple of minutes, the school bus arrived. As I entered, I greeted the bus driver. I can see that Jean and Light were sitting together so I decided to sit beside them. I will try my best not to become the third wheel.

As I was approaching them, suddenly Jean switched places. She went and sat behind.

"Max, come and sit beside me" Light invited.

I was puzzled for a moment.

As I sat beside him I asked "Jean why did you sat behind, aren't you suppose to sit here?"

"No, that is actually your place, I was just sitting there temporarily only" Jean replied. Hmm… okay then if they insist.

"So how was yesterday, did you finish all the assignments?" Light asked.

"UMM…yeah, I only slept at one in the morning thanks to them" I replied.

"Speaking of assignments, may I borrow your chemistry work?" Jean asked Light.

"Jean you are one of the smartest kid in school, how could you not do the assignments?" I asked.

"I am lazy, when my bed calls me, I answer without a blink of an eye" Jean replied.

Lightthen handed his work to Jean as she thanked him with a peck on the cheek.

As we were talking about some stuff, we arrived at our destination which is school. Just like every other Mondays I can't wait for this one to end fast.

When we got down from the bus Jean dragged Light to a corner. I wondered what that was about.

They asked me to head inside first cause they had something to talk about. Without any hesitation, I head in and opened up my locker to put in some of my assignments in there so that I wouldn't lose it.

I looked to my side and I noticed a picture beside it. I've never put a picture in my locker before.

I tried to look closer at the picture and it happened again, what's wrong with me?

It was the same guy with the messy hair and dead eyes.

The picture shows him pointing a gun.

I freaked out for a moment. I tried to calm myself down maybe it was just my imagination. I blinked more than a couple of times and the picture was still there. I immediately took the picture and tossed it into the garbage bin.

As I turned behind I saw the same picture on someone else locker. I look around me and all I see is that same picture. It is everywhere. I ran through the hallway but that picture is everywhere. It is even on some posters through the hall. I ran but it seem like those pictures of him is following me.

His eyes especially seem to be moving according to my movement. I went into the janitor's closet trying to hide from that picture as it freaked me out. I sat in the closet for a while trying to control myself. My heart rate is increasing as it is getting harder for me to breath. I start to pant so hard. It is okay, it is only a hallucination. I tried comforting myself but it isn't working.

After a couple of minutes someone opened the closet. As the brightness entered into the closet, my vision became blur. I tried to adjust my vision as I could see three familiar figures.

It was Light, Jean and Danielle.

"We have been looking everywhere for you" Light stated.

He then gave me a hand and pulled me up onto my foot.

"Are you okay?" Danielle asked.

"Do you want to take the day of?" Jean asked

I manage to calm myself down but as I looked around me all those posters were gone. They look towards I concern.

"I am okay now, I just needed a thinking space that's all" I answered.

"So you chose the Janitor's closet to do those thinking?" Light asked.

"Yeah it is crammed up but it was just perfect" I replied.

They just stared at me and all of the sudden they gave me a big hug. That was a surprise.

"Please don't make us worry about you anymore" Danielle said.

"Yeah, it is like what you said, we are friends. You don't have to hide anything from us" Jean replied.

"We are always here for you" Light stated.

At that moment my heart rate decreases and I stopped panting as hard as before.

A warm smile begins to form on my face. Thank HEAVENS there wasn't anyone in the hall except for us.

"Um… guys, thanks but we could stop hugging now you know. It is getting a bit awkward" I stated.

They soon let go of me and start to chuckle.

"Thanks guys I really needed that" I stated.

They just smiled at me warmly. I am very lucky to have this kind of friends around me.

"Let's head back to our chemistry lab" Light suggested.

"Yeah Mrs. Kina will be mad if we don't enter soon" Danielle insisted.

We all head to the chemistry lab.

As soon as we reached in front of the lab, Light twisted the doorknob clockwise. The door was open and we could see all the students at their respective places. Everyone was just staring at us including Mrs. Kina.

"Where were you guys and why were you all late?" Mrs. Kina questioned us.

"Umm… my locker was stuck and all three of them were helping me to open it" Light answered.

"WHY DIDN'T YOU DO IT AFTER CLASS THEN?" Mrs. Kina questioned again.

Damn she is persistent.

"I would but then I could not submit all the assignments that you have assigned me" Light replied.

Wow! He's really a quick thinker. Mrs. Kina then just pointed at our seats. We all went and sat down at our own respective places. I was sitting beside Light while behind us were Jean and Danielle.

As usual beside us were huge windows which connected us to the outside world. I will not look at windows anymore after what had happened yesterday night in my room.

My thoughts were running wild at that time but Mrs. Kina broke my bubble of thought after she said that we are going to do an experiment today. We wore our goggles and lab coats. Well as usual, I partnered up with Light while Danielle partnered up with Jean.

The experiment involves something about salt and sulfur dioxide.

Well after the experiment, all of us headed to our next class which was English literature.

Again Jean didn't join us and we were all were bored as hell.

As Mrs. Egertson was going on about CLASSIC NOVELS and how we should read them, my phone vibrated.

I slowly took out my phone from my left pocket. It was from Danielle who was sitting two rows behind me. Light too got the message too as I could hear it vibrating from his pocket. Light is sitting beside me.

DANIELLE: Okay, I am really bored over here.

MAXIEL: I thought you love English literature.

DANIELLE: I love the subject not the teacher.

JEAN: Well here I am studying business and I know how it feels.

LIGHT: Well like it or not, it doesn't seem like we have a choice.

JEAN: Light have you given them the tickets yet?

LIGHT: It is in my bag, I plan to do so during recess.

MAXIEL: For the carnival Right?

JEAN: YUP

DANIELLE: Five more minutes till English literature ends.

I placed my phone back into my pocket. Light then bump me on the hand.

"Pssstt… I hope you remember about the football game that you are going to have today" Light notified me. I nodded to him.

Once again thanks to him I had been reminded about stuff that I keep on forgetting.

During recess, we went to the same corner. Light handed in our tickets. I looked at the tickets closely at it says that it is on SEPTEMBER 21st which falls on Wednesday.

"UMM… guys the tickets said that the carnival is on Wednesday" I stated.

Light and Jean were puzzled for a second. He then looked closely onto the date and it states there that it was supposed to be on Wednesday.

"Sorry guys, my bad. Looks like it is only on WEDNESDAY" Light apologized.

"That means you could focus on you football match tomorrow" Danielle stated.

"Yeah we will be on the bleachers rooting for you" Jean said.

I have no idea why but this just made me feel a bit anxious. I mean the whole school is going to be there to watch the match. I just hoped that I would be able to perform tomorrow.

After recess, we head back to or class. I was just looking at the time, thinking about tomorrow. My phone starts vibrating again. This time it was from Light.

LIGHT: MAX, what is wrong? You don't seem to be paying attention.

DANIELLE: YOU OKAY??

MAXIEL: I am fine just thinking about the match tomorrow.

JEAN: Don't worry about that, we will be there for you.

LIGHT: Even the whole school will be rooting for you guys so loosen up will you.

MAXIEL: HAHA… THANKS GUYS.

DANIELLE: Think about the hot girls that you will get after you win the match. You know, I meant me.

LIGHT: Someone has an ego.

I put back my phone in my pocket as it was distracting me from MISS JADE lectures. I don't want to get detention.

As those messages kept on vibrating in my pocket, I was really tempted to look at it but I chose not to. I can't anymore, this is just too tempting so I took out my phone and toss it into my bag so that I couldn't feel any more of those vibrations. I noticed that Light was peeking at my hand to see whether I was using my phone.

He looked surprised as though this was my first time not responding to the group.

As Miss Jade was lecturing us about the HUMAN NERVOUS SYSTEM, my mind suddenly wandered off. It is about the guy with the messy hair and dead eyes. Who was he? Why does he seem a bit familiar? I don't need Light, Jean or Danielle's help to solve this. I could figure this out on my own. I don't want to trouble them like earlier. Even though they had a choice to directly go to Mrs. Kina's class, they chose to search for me. Why am I always troubling them?

After school, I waved goodbye at them and head to the field for football practice. As I entered the locker room, I saw Damian, I wanted to apologize to him but he seemed to be avoiding me. Football practice was going perfect. We even improved our skills.

"Okay guys, tomorrow is a big day. You guys need to get a good night sleep so that you are all able to perform with full potential and stamina tomorrow" coach Langford, advised us.

After the football practice, I tried to find Damian but it seems that he had already left. At the moment my mind is still disturbed about those woods near to the school. I need some answers so that I could stop hallucinating or seeing that girl. So after the practice I directly head to the woods near the school. I need to figure out what is happening.

I searched around the woods for clues but there weren't any. I finally decided to call it a day and head back as soon as I saw the sunset.

One thing that I have learned from movies is that you shouldn't be around the woods during night.

As I reached home, I straight away ran up to my room.

"Don't you want to have dinner first?" my mom yelled.

"It is okay, I don't feel hungry" I replied.

"Well, I will keep it in the refrigerator for you if you want it" she stated.

"Thanks mom" I yelled.

I just feel tired right now. I want to sleep I think being around the woods for hours must have drained my energy.

As I was sleeping it didn't take long before everything went black. It was peaceful until I woke up. When I woke up I realized that I wasn't in my room anymore.

I was in the woods. Right now, I need answers. There must be reasons why this is happening to me. I walked and passed through a couple of trees until I reached the same spot that I always saw the girl in white. This time she wasn't there, I looked around until I saw someone walking through those trees. It was a guy in a uniform, I followed him and what I found out completely shocked me.

As I got a bit deep into the forest, I could see tons of police officers and forensics team around the area.

The dark woods were lighted up with their torchlights.

The only time I remembered there were this many forensics and police was the time during Stacy's murder.

It appears that the people around there could not see me, to them I am a ghost. I could see that some people were carrying a body bag. I approached closer to the body bag. The body bag was halfway zipped.

I leaned nearer to the bag. What I saw in the bag had completely traumatized me. It was Stacy's body.

Her long brown hair was covering half her face. I tried pushing her hair aside so that I could see her face but as I did that, a few of her hair strands got stuck on my hand.

It seems like her body is decomposing but yet it feels weird in a way. Her eyes were halfway closed and all I could see were those dim green eyes just staring at me. Didn't this happen long ago, why am I remembering this now? Her cold body was just sitting in that bag. I noticed something was wrong, in the newspaper it said that there were three gunshots. It should be on her chest, stomach and head but I couldn't spot any gunshots on her body. There wasn't even a drop of blood on her.

I was just staring at her until someone tapped me on the back. I was stunned for a moment as it was the girl in white.

She looked different this time, she was bleeding. Her dress was smothered in blood and her gold necklace that spells out DNIM also has stains of blood.

What happened to her? She held up a gun to my head. I wanted to escape but there was someone who was holding me from behind.

As I looked up it was the man with messy hair and dead eyes. The guy locked my hands so that I couldn't make any movement. At that moment, I felt a bit of current flowing through my body, it felt like I had been electrocuted by something.

As DNIM pulled the trigger, the hammer fell and the bullet hit my head.

Everything just disappeared as the bullet hit my head.

This feeling, I have no idea why but it seems familiar to me.

Looking at Stacy's cold blooded body reminded me of something. Something, that, I want to forget. That feeling of being electrocuted felt familiar too.

The moment I woke up from that nightmare, I immediately took out my phone to search the internet about something. At the search I typed out STACY OTTERCOT. I was astonished to find out that there weren't any details about her. This is weird, why aren't there any results here? There are always results on murder cases on the internet but this time there weren't any.

CHAPTER 13

THE MATCH

I tried sleeping again but it just doesn't seem to work after the nightmare. The time was now a quarter past ten.

I headed downstairs to have my dinner. I took out those leftovers from the freezer and heat it up. After dinner, I soon head back to my bed. I just needed the rest especially for a day like tomorrow. It was easy to fall asleep now.

As I jumped onto my bed, my eyes just closed as if my body was just so tired.

After six hours.

BEEP BEEP, BEEP. That annoying sound is really getting on my nerves. I feel like I could just break the alarm clock right now but I just choose to ignore those feelings.

As usual, waking up in the morning isn't easy. I had to gather up all of my stamina and strength in order to do so.

I got up and did all my usual routine.

I waited outside for the bus to come but this time the bus was ten minutes late. This is the first time that it had ever been late to pick me up. Something is not right today. I looked up to the sky and the weather seems calm. No thunder no lightning roaring throughout the sky.

Today is going to be a good day, I tried to think positive.

As the bus arrived, I got onto the bus. I sat at my usual spot with Light and Jean. It was pretty normal so far and everything seemed to be going as normal.

Everything was normal on our destination to school.

Classes were okay and all but I kept on thinking about the game and how it was going to be? The thought of this bothered me during class so I didn't really paid attention to what I was learning.

As Biology class comes by, Miss Jade was late again. Hmm… this seems to be like her new habit from now but I wasn't complaining. During her lectures, my phone suddenly vibrated. I checked to see who it was and it was from my mom.

MOM: Honey, I won't be able to make it to the game tonight. I am sorry.

MAXIEL: Don't worry about it. It is nothing actually.

I know my mom is busy with her work so I don't really mind since work is one of her main priority.

As I was zoning out in class, I remembered something. Something, about yesterday, the dream that I had, why was there a lot of police officers and forensics team and what does the guy with messy hair and dead eyes have to do with this? Who is he?

I ignored those thoughts and I tried to concentrate on those lectures that Miss Jade was giving. All of a sudden my phone vibrated again. This time I did not pick up. I must start paying attention in class. I don't want to fall behind others.

I looked outside the window and noticed something weird. There is a fruit basket on the grass. Who would leave a fruit basket on the grass?

Some idiot must have forgotten it again. Why would people bring a fruit basket to school? I chose to ignore it.

After school, I had to go home to get some rest since the match is in the late evening.

As I got home, I immediately jumped onto my bed but my eyes could not shut. I guess I'm just nervous.

I picked up my phone and saw the messages that my group was having.

LIGHT: Remember don't be nervous, we will be there to support you.

DANIELLE: Hell yeah we will.

JEAN: Good luck Maxiel, you could do it.

Those messages did make me feel a bit better. I then replied to their messages.

MAXIEL: THANKS GUYS, I APPRECIATE IT!!!

My eyes suddenly felt heavy and I just decided to take a short nap but I did not forget to set up my alarm.

After an hour

BEEP BEEP BEEP. Ughh… an hour had already passed? I got up and decided to take a quick shower to wake myself up.

After getting ready and all, I head towards school. The journey to school was a really long one. I looked up at the sky and noticed that it was getting darker and darker.

As I reached school, I immediately head to the locker room to get changed.

The game will begin in another hour. My teammates were there, we were just chatting about strategy and stuff.

After a couple of minutes coach Langford came in.

"LISTEN UP GUYS, I WANT YOU TO GO OUT THERE AND SHOW THEM WHAT WE ARE MADE OFF!!!" Coach Langford yelled.

Hmm… I was expecting more from a pep talk but I guess that will do for now. We all headed out full of spirit. There were a lot of people on the bleachers. I mean come on this is just some HIGHSCHOOL match.

I could spot Light, Jean and Danielle at the bleachers supporting my team. As the referee blew the whistle, we all strived with aggression towards the other players. My heart was beating fast as I started to run. I got the football and I passed it to Damian. He didn't expect me to pass the ball to him. Damian got a hold of the ball but he seemed a bit distracted. Why is he distracted? This is so not the time to be distracted. Someone tackled Damian and the ball went out of bounce. Luckily our quarter back saved us from losing. DAN is one of the best quarterbacks that I have known. Damian seems like he really is disturbed by something. He could not tackle other players properly.

As the match went on, we had reached the HALFTIME. I looked onto the score board and our teams are tied. I was really out of breath after the first half. I started to pant heavily. We all head back to the locker room because Coach Langford ordered us too. When I was in the locker room, I immediately took my water bottle and drank it. I really need the energy.

"Damian, what is wrong with you today. If you make another mistake, I am going to put you on the bleachers" Coach Langford yelled at him.

He seemed stressed out about something. Before the second half I approached him.

"You okay?" I asked.

He seemed like he doesn't want to talk to me.

"Why do you care? The whole school is going to find out about my secret anyway" Damian stated. His tone of voice was distraught. So that is what he was worried about. I didn't intend to tell anyone. I guess that's why his head isn't in the game tonight.

"Look I didn't tell anyone and I didn't intent to either. Your secret is safe with me" I stated.

"Wait, really you won't?" he asked.

"Yeah, we are bros and bros keep each other's secrets" I replied.

A smile started to form on his face as though a huge burden have been lifted up on his shoulders. He then gave me a huge hug.

"Dude okay, please I like you too but not in the locker room" I squeaked.

He then started to laugh.

"Thanks Maxiel, I really needed that" he stated.

"Now let's go out and have fun okay" I replied.

As we went out, the crowd seemed more active than before. Coach Langford gave us the thumbs up as a sign of good luck. When the referee starts blowing the whistle, I immediately got the ball. I looked around me and all my teammates seemed to be cornered. The only person that I could see was open that time was Damian. Without hesitation, I threw the ball to him. He ran towards the goal and scored a point for all of us.

That means that we are ahead of the other team by a point. We must keep this consistency. The other team managed to score a few points through the game and we made it to the last round. It is a tie again meaning whoever scores this, wins the match.

As the referee blew the whistle, Damian got the ball and he threw it to me. All of my teammates were cornered again meaning that I have to score this one. I was almost tackled by someone but I manage to dodge it. I could hear Light, Jean and Danielle screaming my name out. I ran with all of my strength and stamina towards the goal point. I reached the point before getting tackled by the other players. I did it I scored the final point that is needed to win. Our team cheered up in happiness. The whole crowd gone wild as they started to yell up in happiness. I can't believe it but our team won. This is the first time our team witness victory before our eyes but I mostly felt pain. I should have stretched or warmed up before heading towards the field. My body aches now from all that running. Damn that hurts so badly.

I looked up in the sky and noticed that it is getting cloudy. I saw a flash of lightning. It was beautiful that time, it seems like the dark sky is lighted up by a BLUE light. The team celebrated outside for a while and then we all headed towards the locker room.

Coach Langford was more thrilled then we are. He also complimented on my teamwork with Damian. We celebrated in the locker room. It was fun, everyone was happy. After taking a quick shower, I took out a pair of skinny jeans and a green shirt.

As I got out of the locker room, I could see Light, Jean and Danielle outside waiting for me. They rushed up to me and gave me a big hug. Wow it seems like I am getting a hug from everyone today. We head to the bleachers, the lights were still on but there was no one there.

"Congratulations on your win Light" Jean congratulated me.

"Yeah that final touchdown was amazing" Light said.

I was getting a lot of compliments. It was getting late and it seems that we should head back home.

"I have to go now, I am not going to get a lecture from my parents tonight" Light stated.

"Yeah, sorry I have to go home to" Jean say.

"Well I have to stick around for my driver so see you guys around" Danielle stated.

I don't think it is safe for Danielle to wait alone here.

"It's okay I shall accompany you" I said to Danielle while making eye contact with her.

Light and Jean then got up and started moving towards the exit. We waved them off. So now it is just Jean and me.

"So what time is your driver arriving?" I asked.

Danielle was just making eye contact with me and then she suddenly leaned in closer and gave me a kiss on my lips. I was surprised for a moment, she then pulled back and looked down.

I looked at her in shock.

"I AM SO SORRY" Danielle said.

As she turned to me, I then leaned in closer and kissed her. She pulled back to catch her breath. As she pulled back, her phone vibrated.

"Umm… it is my driver. He is here" Danielle stated.

Too bad cause I really wanted it to happen, I could see the disappointment in Danielle's eyes too.

All of a sudden a smirk form her face. It looks like she had got an idea.

"Hey Maxiel, do you want to stay the night at my place?" she asked.

I was shocked at first when she asked that but as I looked at her, I have a feeling that I was doing the right thing.

"Umm…sure, I would like that" I replied.

She then got up and pulled my hand towards the exit. As we reached at her car the driver was confused about me but he didn't dare to ask. I was sitting beside Daniel in the car.

"Umm… won't your dad ask what I am doing at your place at this hour?" I asked.

"Oh… don't worry about it daddy had gone on a business trip" She stated.

I knew that I had to tell my mom something if not she would be worried about me. I took out my phone and typed a message to her.

MAXIEL: Hey mom, I will be staying the night at Danielle's place today together with Light and Jean. We plan on watching some horror movie.

Okay that should be a good excuse. At that moment I completely forgot that I needed to buy something on the way to Danielle's place.

"Umm.. Danielle, do you mind if we have a quick stop to the convenience store?" I asked.

"Why what do you need to get?" she asked.

"PROTECTION" I answered.

She just nodded at me with some giggling.

"Why what's wrong" I asked.

"Nothing it is just that you are way too straight forward" she answered.

"Louis do you mind if we have a quick stop to the convenience store for a while, my friend here needs to get some bandage for his injury" Danielle lied to the driver.

The driver then nodded.

As we pulled over to the convenience store, I immediately got down of the car and head into the store. I went directly to the aisle where they sold that stuff.

As I went there, I noticed a lot of colorful boxes with logos and stuff. THERE ARE SIZES??? How would I know, this is my first time doing this. I just took the one that is closest to what I think. I then head to the cashier.

As I took out my wallet and looked up, I was stunned.

It was the guy with messy black hair and dead eyes. Those eyes why are they so dim. NO… not this again.

I shook my head left to right and looked up again. This time, it was a guy in red cap and brown eyes. It turns out I think I was hallucinating again. I guess I really needed help but not tonight.

"That will be twenty dollars please" the cashier said as he scanned the item. I took out my wallet and gave him a fifty.

"Alright thank you and here is your change. By the way, enjoy the night kid" he winked at me.

"Umm… thanks" I replied awkwardly.

I guess it is no secret to him about what I am going to be doing tonight.

As I wanted to head out, I just grabbed a pack of bandages too. I went back to the cashier and he seemed pretty confused.

"Hmm… who knew kids these days are into this kind of stuff" he said.

One of my eyebrows lifted up in confusion.

As I paid him he said "Remember be careful, don't hurt yourself" the cashier advised me.

I was so confused on so many levels that I chose to ignore him and head out.

Before I got into the car, I just took out those bandages that I have bought and wave them to the car. I did this so the driver wouldn't think that I was up to no good.

I could see that Danielle was confused by my action but it has to be done.

As I got into the car, Danielle asked me what I was trying to do. I explained to her about that and she started to giggle.

We then arrived to our destination.

I quickly got down of the car followed by Danielle.

"Hold your horses there big guy" Danielle smirked.

She then immediately dragged my hand and brought me to her room.

As we entered into the room Danielle pushed me on top of the bed. The mattress was really soft and cold. My heart beat starts to increase as I started to pant. At that moment I started to think to myself, do I really want to do this? Danielle noticed that I wasn't paying attention to her.

"Hey is everything alright?" Danielle asked.

"Hey Danielle why are we rushing this, I asked.

"What do you mean?" Danielle questioned me.

"Can't we wait, I mean there is really no point in rushing things" I replied.

"Huh…I never hear that often" Danielle replied.

"I'm sorry but there are just a lot of things happening to me right now" I stated.

Danielle looked at me and then starts to giggle.

At that point I was really confused with what is happening.

"You are just too innocent aren't you, I tell you what we will do this slowly and when time comes I hope you will be ready" Danielle replied.

I just nodded at her.

I am glad that I managed to stop it before it goes any further, for some reason I just feel like Danielle is forcing herself to do it.

We should not rush into things like this I want to take my time and get to know Danielle more before I bring our relationship to the next level.

"So what you want to do now?" Danielle asked.

I immediately got up of the bed and took out a movie from her drawer.

"Are you up for it?" I asked.

Danielle just continued to giggle.

"Lead the way" she replied.

Throughout the whole night, we just continued watching movies after movies. We went to bed around four in the morning. I wanted to crash on her sofa but I was too tired to move so I ended up sleeping on her bed.

CHAPTER 14

DINNER AT SEVEN

DRINGGGGGGGGG!!! Danielle's alarm woke me up.

I looked towards the window as the sunbeams were coming through the binds. Danielle was sleeping on my left arm. The alarm only managed to wake her up after a minute.

"Hey there" Danielle says.

I just looked at her with a smile on my face.

"That was one of the longest time that I have stayed up" I said.

"Especially watching a movie throughout the night" Danielle stated.

"Hey could we u…m hang out more often? I asked nervously.

"Sure, I guess this means that we are official huh?"

I nodded at her with a smile.

I got up from the bed and head to the showers. Cold water on a cold morning isn't such a good idea but I need to wake myself up so that I won't feel drowsy. I don't know why but I could not remember any details last night. I am just glad that today was an off day for school.

Our school gave us a day off since we won the football match yesterday. I could hear Danielle watching the news on her flat screen TV.

After I got out of the shower I just wore the same clothes that I came over with since I didn't bring any change of clothes with me.

I jumped onto the bed to watch the MORNING NEWS together with her.

I was surprised to see the man with messy hair and dead eyes on it. The police are apparently searching for him since he committed a murder. The news anchor suggested that if someone spot him, they are required to call the police.

As I blinked again the image turned different. This time it was a dark brown hair male with blue eyes.

This is really starting to get on my nerves. My chain of thoughts were broken as my phone started to vibrate. It was a text message from Light.

LIGHT: Max where are you?

Danielle immediately responded to the text in our group chat.

DANIELLE: He is with me.

LIGHT: Wait why is he with you? Wait never mind I don't want to know.

JEAN: The carnival starts at 8 p.m. but let's meet at 6p.m. so we could have dinner together.

MAXIEL: OKAY!!!

I put down my phone and looked towards Danielle.

"Huh… I guess we are a thing now" I said.

"Aren't we always" Danielle replied.

I looked at her with an intimate eye contact and then gave her a kiss.

"I got to go now so see you at 6 p.m." I excused myself.

Danielle just looked at me with a big smile on her face. I just smiled back and exited her room then.

As I reached at the bottom of the staircase, I tried avoiding the maids and butlers there. Luckily I managed to avoid everything. I guess they must be busy preparing for something important.

After I sneaked my way out of the house, I could see Danielle waving at me from her balcony. I then waved back at her as I turned back and kept moving forward.

On my way home, I looked up at the sky and it was starting to turn cloudy. I guess it must be a rainy season since it is starting to rain now and then.

As I got home, I could see my mom watching television.

"Why didn't you go to work?" I asked.

"Ohh... I took the day off" she replied.

I head to the kitchen to grab a bite since I didn't have my breakfast yet. I opened the fridge and looked.

I found some bread and cheese. Hmm... that should do. I did my own breakfast this time.

"So how was yesterday, did you have fun?" my mom asked.

I looked down in embarrassment as all those thoughts went through my head.

"It was fun" I replied.

I then headed upstairs. Something tells me that today is going to be one of those days that I would not forget. I am sure that I will have tons of fun with them at the carnival. I can't wait for tonight.

I tilted my head to look at the time and it points at a quarter past eleven. The sky begun to drizzle as the wind became much stronger. I hope it doesn't rain tonight.

I need a short nap. I know that I have been sleeping a lot lately but I think I used up most of my stamina last night and the weather is also tempting me.

It is nice to sleep during a rainy weather.

As I was about to lie down on my bed, I noticed something was sticking out of the closet, it looks like a piece of paper. Where did that come from? I leaned in closer and picked it up with my right hand.

As I looked closer, it was a photograph of Light, Jean, Danielle and me. It was a bit faded. I know that I am in it but I could not recognize the background. The background was filled with colorful bright lights. Huh… maybe this happened some time ago that is why it was faded. I just could not recall the place or recognize the background.

I tried not to think too much about it. I just put it onto my desk and immediately jumped onto my bed.

I lay on my bed, the weather just made me sleepier as it got heavier and heavier. My eyelids just shut and everything went black. It was peaceful. There isn't anything to disturb me while I am sleeping well except for those horrible dreams that I had.

BEEP BEEP BEEP My alarm woke me up. I was still a bit cranky and I accidentally hit it.

The alarm fell onto the ground and broke.

As the alarm fell onto the ground, a high pitched sound suddenly appeared.

It hurts my ears as I screamed in agony.

As I got my body up, the sound just vanished. What was that? That frequency just hurts my ears. It made me feel like my ears were bleeding out. I tried to think what that was but it doesn't make any sense.

I got up of bed and noticed that the photograph wasn't on the table anymore. I was puzzled. I looked all around including under the table and almost the whole room but there wasn't anything.

Where could that photograph be?

As my head was filled with this flow of thoughts, my phone suddenly vibrated. It was a text from Jean.

JEAN: Are you guys ready?

I looked at the time it was a quarter past five. I have forty-five minutes to get ready. My phone vibrated again and this time it was a text from Danielle.

DANIELLE: YUP!!!

LIGHT: We shall meet at our school.

JEAN: Is everyone okay with it? Maxiel where are you?

MAXIEL: Yeah sure, I will meet you guys there at six.

I wondered why school? This is the first time that we were actually meeting up near school.

Normally we meet up at someone's house or something. I should not think too much of this. I headed for the showers and took a long refreshing bath.

As I got out, I immediately took out a grey shirt and a dark brown pair of skinny jeans. I wore a read hoodie on my grey shirt.

I then headed out to school. Apparently my mom had gone out somewhere so I left a note on the fridge indicating that I will be home late.

As I got out, I noticed the clouds have gone darker and the weather is getting colder.

It was so cold that I had to zip up my hoodie and placed my hands in my pocket. I crave for warmth at that moment. I need something to keep me warm. My phone started buzzing all of a sudden. It was a text from Danielle.

DANIELLE: I am already at school, where are you guys?

JEAN: We are on our way.

MAXIEL: Same here.

I placed the phone back into my pocket as I kept on walking.

It took me about twenty minutes to reach there.

As I was walking, I was completely shocked as someone ran towards me and hugged me from behind. I was ready to defend myself but it was just Light.

"Woah… chill out dude" Light said.

Jean was way behind him waving at me.

As I looked forward, I noticed Danielle's car and her driver.

My guess is that she doesn't want to stand in this cold. He soon got out of her car and waved to the driver as she saw us.

"You guys are so late" Danielle said in frustration.

We apologized to her and she just nodded at us.

"Come on there is a western restaurant near by" Light stated.

We all head towards the restaurant to have dinner. We were all having some small chats. We were just too excited for the carnival. We took an hour at the restaurant and now we are going to the spot.

Only Light and Jean knew where it is being held. Danielle and me are kind of blur at the moment as they took us to school.

"We have to cross these woods in order to reach the carnival. It is on the other side" Light stated.

Isn't there another way? Why must it always be near the woods of the school?

"Maxiel, are you afraid" Jean teased me with a smirk.

"No, No I am not" I stammered.

The truth is I am a bit afraid after all those incidents. Even the weather is scary right now. It is all so dark and cloudy. I managed to take a deep Breath and followed them to the woods. It took us like fifteen minutes in order to reach to the other side.

CHAPTER 15

COLORFUL NIGHT

Once we were on the other side, we could see colorful lights all around us.

It was like the sky had been lighted up by a giant disco ball.

The view was just so beautiful; it's like being a child all over again. I felt some mild breeze around me.

I suddenly had a weird feeling. I looked up to the sky and noticed a thick cloud circulating around the carnival. It is like something big is going to go down tonight. Whatever this feeling that I am having, I have to ignore it for their sake.

I have been overthinking for a long time now, maybe I should just enjoy my time with them and ignore my surroundings. We head to the counter to show our entry tickets to a lady in uniform.

Once we were in, there were a bunch of stuff like the carousel, roller coaster and other fun stuff.

"Come on we are heading to the roller coaster first" Danielle dragged my hand as I blurred out for a moment.

There is one weird fact about the carnival that I noticed.

There aren't a lot of people there and I considered that weird. I expected this place to be crowded but something just feels wrong for some reason.

The line for the roller coaster wasn't long. We got on it after just a couple of seconds waiting in line. What is going on here? Maybe people don't know that there is a carnival being held here or maybe they are just busy.

As we sat on our seats on the roller coaster, my heart started to pound hard. Danielle was sitting beside me while Light and Jean were sitting together at the back of us. How bad could this be right? It then started to move and this is when my heart starts pounding even harder.

As we ascend into the sky, my thoughts were thinking on how this could go wrong? I tried to calm myself down but when we reached that high from the ground, my thoughts were on how screwed I was.

The cart stopped for a while in the air. I was not sure whether this is supposed to make us enjoy the view or prepare ourselves for the worst to come?

There was a beep sound this indicates that the cart is going to descend. I took a deep breath as the cart was about to descend.

After five seconds, it descended so fast that Danielle's hair starts to block Light's view. It is already scary riding in a roller coaster but imagine riding it blind. We were all screaming for our lives as the cart goes in hoops and turns. It feels like forever when I was on the cart.

As we arrived at the end point of the roller coaster, I was pretty sick. I felt like throwing up but I managed to get a hold of myself. I think this is going to be the last time I am going to ride a roller coaster.

We took a five minute break before jumping onto the next ride.

"Let's go onto the carousel next" Jean suggested while dragging Light.

I noticed that Light had still not recovered from the ride yet but he managed to suck it in for Jean.

As we arrived at the carousel, there weren't even a single person around that area. It was just the carousel moving at its own speed. I did not think much about it and jumped and hopped onto it with the others. Jean and Danielle were sitting on the white horses while Light and me were just standing there trying not to get dizzy. I guess I still haven't recovered from the previous ride before.

At that moment, I suddenly noticed a flash of light.

That completely got me off guard. Maybe it was just the lightning. I ignored the flash since it could just be my imagination. Danielle was doing some stupid poses with her horse until at one point, she fell off it. We burst out in laughter as we saw what happened to her.

"Gee… you guys sure are good friends" Danielle said in sarcasm.

She was still on the platform of the carousel as it was still rotating.

"Sorry, I just can't control myself. I mean it is your fault for not watching out" Light stated.

I held my hand out to Danielle to help her out. She grabbed my hand and pulled herself up.

"Okay I think we are done with the carousel, where should we go next?" Danielle asked.

All of us hopped back down from the rotating platform carefully. I looked around and I noticed that there was something called THE HOUSE OF MIRRORS.

"Let's go there" I suggested while pointing to the place.

"Sure why not" Light replied.

Danielle and Jean just nodded at us while we all head towards the House of mirrors. It is getting really weird now. There were less and less people around here as time passed by.

There weren't anyone around the House of mirrors. It was quite lonely.

We were standing outside the place when Danielle said "You guys go ahead first, I want to check on something".

"Should I accompany you?" I asked.

"No, it's okay. This is something personal" Danielle shook her head.

"What could you do that is personal here? Are you going to make out with a clown?" Light smirked.

Danielle just rolled up her eyes and left. The three of us then entered the place. It was way bigger than I thought it would be. It was literally a maze made out of mirrors. The whole place was a bit dim. They did put up directions at every corner in case someone got lost.

"Hey Maxiel, do you mind being here alone for a while?" Jean asked with a smirk on her face.

"Um… yeah sure, no problem" I replied.

Jean then dragged Light into a corner. I was just looking around until I saw a reflection of them making out. I don't need to see that.

I walked around until I stumbled upon a white piece of paper.

As I turned the white piece of paper around, my heart starts pounding really hard. The words YOU DON'T BELONG HERE is written in blood on that paper. No… not this, not now. I turned around searching for Light and Jean but I stumbled upon the guy with messy hair I was stunned for a moment.

"It is time boy, you don't belong here" the man stated.

He took out a gun out of his left pocket. A cunning smile starts to form on his face as he did so.

I tried to escape by pushing him but when I did, my hand just went pass through him. No, this can't be happening. What is he? I turned around to run away but behind me there stood the girl in white. She was blocking my path.

"You can't escape fate" she muttered in a soft and calm tone of voice.

I turned back to look at the man but he completely vanished. How did he do that? Where is he? I turned back in front to look at the girl. I was completely shocked as I saw her standing in front of me. She looked so different this time. Both her blonde hair and white dress had suddenly turned black. Her beautiful yellow iris had now turned blood red. Her soft fair skin had turned pale.

I looked into her eyes, it was filled with bloodlust. I knew that it was her since I could still see that gold necklace that spells out DNIM hanging around her neck.

It was getting hard for me to breathe as my heart rate increased. My heart was pounding like crazy. I started to shiver as I do not know what I am facing right now.

She suddenly lifted up her right hand that was holding something sharp. I looked closer and I noticed that her hand had turned into sharp claws. She was ready to strike me. I closed my eyes preparing for the worst.

I really find it hard to breathe at the moment, I was panting really hard.

"Maxiel, Maxiel are you alright" I heard that voice in front of me.

As I opened my eyes, I noticed that Danielle was standing in front of me. The girl or whatever it was had disappeared. She just vanished just like that. I was still panting really hard.

"Are you okay?" Danielle asked.

I managed to calm myself down.

"Yeah, I…I'm alright" I stammered.

I looked at Danielle and noticed that she was carrying something. It was pink and fluffy. It was cotton candy the way she held it was kind of funny.

She seems to be struggling to hold all four of those. Did she just separated from us to get cotton candy? For a second there I kind of forgot everything and started to laugh.

"Wow you are such a gentleman, thanks for helping me carry these" Danielle stated sarcastically.

"No… I didn't mean to laugh" I calmed myself down and then helped her to carry two of those cotton candies.

"Where are Light and Jean?" Danielle asked.

"They are currently over there sharing saliva" I replied.

"LIGHT, JEAN I GOT COTTON CANDIES" Danielle yelled.

Out of nowhere they suddenly appeared behind us. Wait how did they get behind us? I guess they were exploring in their own ways.

Danielle handed them the cotton candy and they look a bit surprised. This pink cotton candy that I held in my hand brought back some memories of my childhood.

What disturbs me the most was what had happened to me?

CHAPTER 16

HEARTBROKEN TRUTH

After we browsed around the area with our cotton candies, we decided to head back home.

I looked up and noticed that there was a huge clock hanging up there. It was a quarter past ten.

"We should hurry up" Danielle said.

Light and Jean nodded.

Something feels odd, I just feel very uneasy at the moment. I looked up to the sky and notice a strike of lightning. The moon was covered by a thick layer of clouds.

The air around me grew colder and colder as we left the carnival, The whole carnival shut down after we left the area. The colorful sky was now engulfed by darkness.

"It's okay, it will be quick" Light said as he pointed to the woods.

At that moment, the only thing that lighted up the darkness was the lightning that's soaring through the sky.

My heartbeat starts to increase. This feeling of uneasiness just became worst. I was just following Light and the others. They seem to know where to go in this darkness.

It seems like they had memorized the whole area.

After a couple of seconds, we suddenly STOP walking.

"Why did we stop walking? Is everything okay?" I asked.

There weren't any reply.

Darkness still surrounds the area but I could roughly see what was going on.

Then it happened, a strike of lightning just passed by and I could see the same cliff where I met DNIM.

My jaw dropped to the ground as I was puzzled at the moment.

Light was leaning on the rock while Danielle and Jean were standing beside him. They were just staring at me with guilt in their eyes.

Why are they just sitting there? Why aren't we moving?

"Hey guys why aren't we heading home?" I asked.

"We just wanted to hang out here for a while though" Light replied.

The clouds were blown a bit, revealing a full moon.

The moon lighted up the place but there was still lightning surrounding the area.

"Could we not hang around the place where Stacy died?" I asked.

It is really not comfortable hanging at a place where a teenage girl was brutally murdered.

Light approached me with a smile on his face. He was calm but guilty in a way.

"Stacy didn't die here" Light said.

"What do you mean, of course Stacy died here" I insisted.

Light took a deep breath and gave me full eye contact.

"Stacy died of her sickness" replied Light.

I was really confused at the moment. They looked as though their whole world had been torn apart.

"I know someone was murdered here, I remembered seeing the police all over this place"

Light then walked back to Danielle and Jean. They were standing in a group only I was the one that was isolated by them.

"Someone was murdered here but it wasn't Stacy, it was us" Light replied.

My heartbeat increases as I heard those words came out.

"What do you mean? Guys you stop joking around. Let's go home" I said while panting really hard.

After saying those words I suddenly felt as though I was electrocuted. I held my hand upon my heart trying to calm myself down.

Light approached me again.

"Max, you were like a brother to me. We always looked out for each other and do stupid stuff together".

"Where are you going with this Light?" I interrupted him.

He just looked at me with a smirk on his face.

"I'm going nowhere. Something tells me that we could have been best bros when we grow up but it seems life have other plans" Light sighed in despair.

I looked at him in confusion but my eyes were starting to tear up. It seems like I knew what had happened but wasn't willing to accept it.

After Light said those words, blood started dripping from his mouth. I looked at him and noticed a gunshot to his chest.

"Guess my time is up. It's okay you were always tough on your own" Light smirked.

He then positioned himself leaning to the rock near the cliff and closed his eyes.

No, what is happening? Jean then approached me and stood in front of me.

"We knew that you could not accept the pressure of this that is why we decided to relive these precious moments that we had with you. It is also our way of saying goodbye to you" Jean stated. I suddenly noticed the tears that were rolling down her face.

"No… pl…please don't g…go" I stammered I felt like I was losing my voice.

Jean then tried to fake a smile. It is hard to fake a smile when you are really sad.

"Look Greene... it's okay. You should not hang onto us; it's time to let us go. I will miss you a lot. Cheer up, you still a long way to go" Jean stated that while hitting my shoulder lightly.

Blood starts to drip out of her stomach. It was a gunshot to her stomach. She then went and positioned herself next to Light.

Her eyes weren't closed. It was dead open. I looked towards Danielle as tears starts rolling down my face.

"No... Danielle please don't" Danielle approached me.

She was one step closer to me then Light and Jean. She looked down trying to avoid eye contact

After a couple seconds of silence, she then looked up to me.

"I tried my best to control my tears but I just can't" her tone of voice was soft as tears were all over her face.

"I really liked you a lot. You were the only person I felt connected with in life. My only regret was not spending enough time with you and not telling you about how much I love you". She then leaned closer and gave me a kiss on my lips. Her kiss was filled with love and warmth.

Out of a sudden, she pushed me.

As I was sliding down the woods, I heard a loud gunshot. I looked up and saw a bullet hit Danielle's head as she collapsed onto the ground.

"NO…PLEASE DON'T" I yelled as kept on flowing down my face.

As those words came out of me, I hit something big and hard.

CHAPTER 17

FORGOTTEN TRUTH

BEEP BEEP BEEP.

I woke up in shock as my head hit something.

I looked around me and noticed that I was surrounded by some people. I couldn't see them clearly since my vision is still adjusting to the bright light that surrounds the room.

WHAT IS HAPPENING? WHERE AM I?

After my vision became much clearer, I noticed that I was surrounded by doctors and nurses.

One of the doctors was holding a defibrillator. They looked happy to see me awake.

My chest was wet and it still hurts a bit.

What's going on? One of the doctors then approached me and grabbed my shoulder

"Everything is just going to be alright".

I was puzzled for a moment.

A woman with glasses and white coat suddenly appeared and approached me. It was my mom. She leaned in closer to me and gave me a warm hug.

"Honey you have just woken up from a coma. I thought I was going to lose you".

I looked at her with my eyes wide open.

"How long was I out?" I asked.

"You were in a coma for approximately two months. When your vitals started to drop, we panicked and used the defibrillator on you" she replied.

I looked up at the television that was hanging onto the walls in the room.

It showed a familiar face. It was the man with the messy hair and dead eyes. There was a headline below his picture stated MASS MURDER OF THREE TEENS.

"Mom where's Danielle, Light and Jean?" I asked in a soft tone.

She then looked at me in despair and gave me a hug. It then hit me. Everything make sense now, all my memories came swarming back to me.

It was about the night we tried to pass through the woods as a shortcut.

There was a man who suddenly stopped us and pointed a gun at Light. He then shot Light in the chest followed by Jean in her stomach. Then Danielle may have pushed me in order to save me and I saw her got shot in her head. I saw the killer it was the man with the messy hair and dead eyes.

Why didn't I do anything that time? Why was I so useless?

These thoughts of rage and despair just came gushing through my mind. I knew I should have done something but what is the point of regretting it now?

It was already too late.

I looked up at my mom in despair. Everyone in the room left, only leaving my mom and me

"Honey, you should be discharged in three days" she said.

I can't get over the murder of Danielle, Light and Jean.

"Mom can I have some time alone please" I asked.

"Sure of course, take your time. If you need anything just press the blue button" my mom stated.

She then left the room. I noticed a basket of fruits tied with purple ribbon. I got up of my bed and approached the basket of fruits.

My mind still couldn't cope with the current situation. On the purple ribbon, there was a white card with golden highlights tied to it. It states

HEY MAXIEL, IT IS JUST BORING OVER HERE WITHOUT YOU. HOPE YOU GET UP SOON. It was signed by Elle.

I am not sure how to feel at the moment. I just feel so empty right now as I lay my head onto a pillow.

My thoughts were just trying to process the things that had just happened to me. It took me a couple of minutes to cope up with life. I then pressed the button.

"Yes honey, do you need anything?" my mom came rushing in.

"Can I be discharged now?" I asked.

She looked at me in anger.

"You need to rest" her tone of voice was a bit rough.

"Please mom, I have already lost two months of my life" I said it in frustration.

She looked at me in hesitation.

"Are you sure?" she asked.

I nodded.

I was discharged in the evening. My mom sent me home after she had done with her shift. We were quiet in the car; I didn't make any conversations with her.

As soon as we reached home, I immediately went up to my room. I jumped onto my bed and lay my head on the pillow. I was tired even though I had two months of rest. I set my alarm for school. My eyes just went heavy and it closed after a few seconds. I was lying on a pile of darkness but for some reason, I really miss this feeling.

After two hours.

DRIIIINGGGGG!!! My alarm rang as I woke up to shut it.

Why is my face wet? I touched my cheeks and noticed that it was my tears.

I guess I still miss them.

I immediately head to the bathroom to wash off the sorrows that my face had left.

I took a cold shower as usual.

After I came out of the shower I took out a black shirt with a pair of black skinny jeans.

I grabbed my phone and looked at the time and date. Huh… now is November 22nd. It was already a quarter past six I the morning.

I was too tired to look at the date yesterday. I guess I finally coped up with time.

I head downstairs and saw my mom making breakfast.

She looked at me in shock "Are you sure that you want to go to school today?"

"Yeah, sooner or later I have to go anyway, so I don't really mind" I replied.

I sat down and just stared at the bacon and eggs that my mom had prepared.

I really had no appetite to eat but I forced myself.

"Well I am on my way to work so why not I send you to school directly" my mom offered.

I just nodded.

As I was putting on my shoes, I noticed an old newspaper on the rack. I was shocked to find out that it has Danielle, Light and Jean pictures on it. It states MASS MURDER OF THREE TEENAGERS CULPRIT WAS FOUND. LOCAL TEEN GIRL HELPED TO JUSTIFY THE INCIDENT.

The guy who murdered them was known as BILL OTTERCOT.

He was high on drugs the night he committed the murder. He was sentenced to lifetime in prison.

If only he didn't do drugs, they would still be alive but I can't change anything now can't I?

"Are you ready?" my mom asked.

"Yea, I am" I replied.

On our way to school I had this thoughts running through my mind about how it's never going to be the same again.

As we arrived to our destination, my heartbeat starts to increase. I was a bit nervous.

"Enjoy your day" my mom said as I closed the car door.

At the compound everyone looked at me weirdly as though I was the kid who had woken up from the dead.

All of a sudden someone hugged and lifted me up from behind.

"Hey bro, how are you doing?" I looked behind me and noticed that it was Damian and his friends. I was currently surrounded by jocks.

"Yeah I am fine, thanks for asking" I replied.

I know that they are trying to be friendly and all but I was a little bit uncomfortable.

After a couple of chats with them, I finally entered into the school building. Everyone kept looking at me and that just made me feel even more insecure.

I grabbed the books that I needed and immediately head to class.

As I entered into my class I was shocked by a loud voice that yelled out my name.

"MAXIEL!" It was Elle, she came rushing towards me and gave me a huge hug.

"Hey Elle" I said.

I looked across my classroom and noticed the three tables that were unoccupied.

"Huh… so they are really gone" I whispered that to myself.

Elle must have heard me as she immediately let go of the hug.

"Hey um… if you want we could visit the cemetery after school" Elle suggested.

"Yes I would like that" I replied.

She then went to her seat. I sat down at that same old place that I have been sitting for a long time but this time it just felt so different.

I just felt that I was missing a part of me.

After a few seconds of just staring outside the window, I remembered DNIM.

Who is she?

I still haven't figured out that part yet.

All of a sudden Miss Jade came in.

"Ah... Maxiel, it is nice to see that you could join us today" Miss Jade smiled at me.

I just nodded and smiled back at her.

"Okay class today we are going to learn about the nervous system" Miss Jade stated.

I wasn't really paying attention to her, I was just thinking about all the stuff that had happened to me in the last two months.

Suddenly, a girl came into our class.

"Yes Linda could we all know why are you late today?" Miss Jade asked.

Who is that girl? I haven't seen her before.

"Um… my car broke down" the girl replied.

Miss Jade just pointed her to the seat next to me.

I guess she must be new here. She approached the desk beside me and sat there.

That is where Light would normally sit. She took Light's place and that just made me depressed

I still couldn't cope with me losing them. Right now my thoughts were still processing reality. I know that I was in a coma for two months. In my mind, I was still trying to figure out who is this DNIM character and how she was involved in all of this?

The girl who sat beside me is currently putting make up on her face. I started to scribble DNIM's name on a piece of paper.

Out of a sudden, the girl beside me dropped her mirror and it shattered to pieces. The whole class was looking at her. Her face became bright red as everyone started to giggle.

"Sorry, I was clumsy. I will clean that up" Linda apologized.

"Well you should and please stop distracting my class" Miss Jade said.

Miss Jade then continued her lecture as the girl carefully picked up a few of the broken glasses. I bend down to help her pick up those shattered glasses.

"Thanks my name is Linda by the way" she said.

I just smiled and nodded at her.

The piece of paper that I had scribbled DNIM's name must have slipped and fell onto the ground.

The paper had landed over a piece of the broken mirror.

"HUH… why did you write MIND on a piece of paper?" Linda asked.

I was confused for a second. When I picked it up, I was shocked to find out that it spelled MIND on the mirror.

All of a sudden, it gave me an idea who DNIM is or was? Light once told me that sometimes our subconscious could act as a defend mechanism when we are in trouble. Could the girl in white dress known as DNIM actually be my subconscious trying to get me out of my coma?

Why haven't I realized this before? DNIM spelled backwards is M…I…N…D. DNIM was actually trying to get me out of my coma no wonder she kept on saying that I don't belong here.

Her actions also justify this since she randomly pops up at random places in random times.

It also explains how she could handle the cold weather while wearing only a thin layer of clothing.

After I helped Linda to clean up the broken glasses, I went back to my seat. Huh… I guess I could remember some things that Light told me. It is kind of depressing to know that I would never have that again.

Throughout the entire day of school, I wasn't really paying attention in class.

I was just scrolling through the messages that Danielle, Light, Jean and me had before they were murdered. It was sad to kept on thinking about it.

I know that it's no use crying or grieving over them since they are already dead but I just can't help myself.

After our school bell rang, Elle approached me.

"Are you ready?" She asked in a soft tone.

I nodded at her.

We then headed outside the school. I could see an orange sports car with black stripes on it. I am guessing that it is Elle's car and sure enough I was right.

The entire journey was just us listening to pop songs on the radio.

I looked at the back of the car and noticed three bouquets of roses.

As we arrived at our destination, I was panting really hard.

"It's okay, I know it isn't easy but you will have to accept it sooner or later" Elle said.

I got out of the car and noticed that it was cloudy. There weren't much grave stones over there. There were three grave stones that stood out overall.

Elle was walking in front of me while carrying all three of the bouquet of flowers. Something stopped me as I saw a man with a suit standing in front of one of the grave stones.

I just ignored this feeling that I was having and continued to follow Elle.

As I got closer and closer to the man I suddenly noticed who he was, it was Mr. Fond.

Mr. Fond noticed us and gave us a warm smile.

As we stood in front of the three grave stones, Elle laid a bouquet of roses on each grave stone.

"Thank you" Mr. Fond thanked Elle.

Elle just nodded at him with a smile. Light's gravestone was in the middle of Danielle's and Jean's.

"Oh! Maxiel just hold on for a moment. I forgot I left something in the car".

As Elle left, it was just Mr. Fond and me standing in front of the grave stones. It was quiet for a moment and then suddenly I noticed tears started to roll down from his face.

I decided to keep quiet. All of a sudden Mr. Fond said

"This whole thing, it is all my fault".

At that moment I was puzzled. What did he meant when he said it was his fault?

"I am sorry Maxiel, it was my fault that you have lost your friends, it was also my fault that I lost my beloved daughter" Mr. Fond muttered.

"What do you mean Mr. Fond?" I asked curiously.

Mr. Fond looked at me as he tried to control himself. His deep blue eyes were filled with regret and hatred.

"Bill Ottercot was one of my employees and he was also a single father" he said.

At that moment I completely froze.

"Maxiel do you know a girl by the name of Stacy?" he asked me.

What does this have to do with Stacy? My head was running with thoughts.

"Yeah she was a senior at my school" I replied with a humble tone.

"Stacy passed away of Leukemia over three months ago" my mind was still trying to process all of these information as I was also trying to figure out how is this Mr. Fond's fault?

"My company faced some downfalls over seven months ago, so we had to let go of a few employees. This includes Bill Ottercot. Bill tried to beg for his job back after the charity ball since he really needed the money in order to pay for Stacy's hospital bill. He got upset when I denied him and that's when he broke one of my vases. At that moment I chased him out of my house in anger. I should have listened to him. He sold his house and car in order to keep up with the payments but when he could not do so, the doctors decided to stop giving Stacy her medications".

"Mr. Fond, this couldn't possibly be your fault" I tried to calm him down but then tears starts to roll down his cheeks again.

"I hired a personal investigator to check on Bill. I found out that he got addicted to drugs after Stacy's death. I guess he couldn't face the reality that he had lost his daughter. He blamed me for what had happened to Stacy. He probably thought that if he couldn't have his daughter then why should I. I guess that is when he started targeting Danielle. I rushed over when I heard the news but I was already too late" Mr. Fond explained.

"But then why would he target Light, Jean and me?" I asked.

Mr. Fond just looked over at me and said

"I guess he was stalking you guys for some time now. When you guys entered into the woods, he figured out it was the best opportunity to kill Danielle since there weren't anyone around. Maybe he wanted to kill the three of you since he doesn't want any witnesses. No one knows this story except me and now probably you. When the police caught him they found that he was under the influence of drugs and that is why they put it in the newspaper without actually investigating the true story" Mr. Fond stated.

I can't make any eye contact with Mr. Fond at the moment since I know it was his fault but I can't also jump to conclusions since he only did what was best for his company.

I felt bad for Bill Ottercot but at the same time I still couldn't forgive him for taking away three of my best friends.

"Now I know how Bill felt" Mr. Fond said as he left trying to contain his tears from rolling down his face.

Now it was only me there.

After a couple of seconds Elle came back.

"I am sorry I was late, it took me a while to search for it" Elle said.

I was just sad that I couldn't meet them anymore. If only Mr. Fond did not fire Bill then this probably would not had happened.

Elle noticed that I was in devoured by despair.

"I know how you feel Maxiel" Elle said.

There was a short pause between us for a moment and then she handed me something. It was a photograph of us at the carousel.

"I was there when everything went down. I saw them get murdered".

I was stunned when I heard that.

"What did you meant by that Elle?" I asked.

"I was following you guys from behind all along. I wanted to surprise you guys in the woods but when I saw that guy appeared with the gun, I decided to hide. I saw everything, after Bill shot them, he suddenly panicked. It looks like he had just done something that he regretted. He then dropped the gun and immediately ran away. I saw how Danielle pushed you to save your life. I was the one who discovered you when you had fainted. I also called for help that day. When you were in coma, I was one of the witnesses in court who justified against the murder." Elle stated in despair.

She looked down on the grave trying to avoid making eye contact with me.

I was stunned for a moment.

"I…if on..ly I had do…done s…something" she stammered.

She was trying her best to control her tears.

I immediately grabbed her hand and held it tightly.

"It's okay, maybe this was meant to be. Everything happens for a reason right?" I said.

Elle just nodded at me.

All of a sudden tears started to roll down my face. Huh… I guess I am still not over them yet. All of the memories of us together suddenly started flowing through my mind.

My tears started dripping over their grave stones. No matter how hard I try to control myself, I just couldn't stop. If only I had done something or even cancel going to the carnival that day, this could have been prevented.

I know all friendships must come to an end but I wish our friendship didn't have to end like this.